Off Limits

SABRINA DEVLIN

Acknowledgements:

First and foremost to my wonderful husband who has always been my biggest supporter. He is my knight in shining armor and my prince charming all wrapped in one.

Also to my son and the twins who make life worth living.

Last, but not least, thank you to Renee, my editor, and to Small Mammoth Design at smallmammothdesign.com for the cover.

Chapter 1

Not again! That was all Amanda Harrington could think as she caught her first glimpse of the instructor sitting at the table outside the room she'd been assigned to at the gym. Her steps faltered for just a moment as reality hit that it really was none other than Jake Marshall signing in students. She couldn't believe she was getting the same physical training instructor she'd had the last time she'd been at the academy. What were the odds of that happening? Whatever they were, they obviously weren't in her favor. Oh well. Might as well get it over with, Amanda thought as she headed over to the sign in table.

"Last name?" asked Jake Marshall, not even bothering to lift his head from scanning the roster sheet.

"Harrington," replied Amanda.

Jake looked up in response to the husky, yet obviously female tone of voice. For a moment he thought his eyes were deceiving him. It was the same woman he'd had in his class just last year!

"Don't I know you?" Jake asked.

"Nice line," Amanda answered. Jake frowned and thought back to the last time he'd had her in his class. She'd had a big chip on her shoulder then. Guess not much had changed.

"Nice attitude," was Jake's reply and Amanda felt herself turning red. Great. She'd been trying for a little levity, but as soon as she'd said the words she wished she could take them back. She wasn't very good when it came to having a quick come back. Oh, she could come up with the perfect one...it was always just ten seconds too late.

Nice start to the twelve weeks of hell she was going to have to endure here at the academy.

"Start stretching out on the mats," Jake told her, indicating the doorway behind him as he continued on to the next person in line.

So, here she was back at the Federal Law Enforcement Training Center, commonly referred to as the "academy" by the law enforcement personnel that were trained there. It was her second time around in just over a year, this time for criminal investigator training. She was still with the same agency, under the Department of Homeland Security, and probably shouldn't have been too surprised to have the same instructor again. Most of the instructors taught at the academy for two years and she was returning within that time frame. Logically it all made sense since each agency hired its own instructors, but having Jake Marshall as her physical training instructor again was still a shock. She just hadn't prepared herself for that possibility.

Jake Marshall had been the bane of her existence. He'd put her through the wringer her first time at the academy and she still considered it a miracle that she'd survived. She started having flashbacks to the last time she had him as an instructor. Tapping into any memories from her first time at the academy was something she'd been hoping to avoid, but just the few that came to mind had her quaking inside. She just knew she was going to get her butt kicked every day by this guy again for the next three months. The guy thought he was a military drill sergeant with the way he'd yelled at her previous class. It had been relentless. Joy. She was going to get to go through that all over again.

Well, at least he remembered me, thought Amanda as she was stretching on the padded floor of one of the many mat rooms at the gym. Being in a mat room sure brought back some bad memories. Padded floors and padded walls didn't conjure up anything good. She'd considered the mat rooms torture chambers last time. Where else do you have many identical, windowless, fully padded, lockable rooms down a long hallway? At an insane asylum for sure, and yet here she was back at the academy!

Seeing that Jake was going to be her instructor again brought up all the negative feelings she'd tried to put behind her before coming back. She figured she must have left some sort of impression on him. Now she was just going to worry if it was good or bad. Probably pretty bad. Her last time here at the academy had been rough. She hadn't really known what to expect and remembered feeling like a fish out of water. She'd been really out of shape, at least as far as being able to keep up with the unexpected military style boot camp. She'd expected the physical training to help her reach a new level of fitness...in a civilized manner. Her mistake. It had been more like the hell week she'd once seen on television when new recruits started out in the army. Imagine grown men puking up their breakfast after a ton of push-ups and people collapsing by the side of the road during a road march. She had been shell-shocked. The running in formation for miles along with being pushed to the limit in all other exercises had really taken its toll. She'd felt so beaten up every day that half of the time she didn't know how she'd made it through the rest of her classes.

Things were going to be different this time around though. Sure, Jake Marshall was a stumbling block she hadn't expected. She had been hoping to start with a clean slate, not knowing anyone and no one knowing her. No matter though, this time around she was here to kick some ass. At least that's what she had to keep telling herself. Attitude played an important part in winning the battle around here. She remembered from last time that it didn't pay to let them see you sweat. Those who complained just got worked over harder.

Little did she know that Jake was already berating himself for the way he'd handled things. He felt like he must have stared at her for a full minute with his mouth hanging open after she'd said her last name. And had he really said that awful line? She'd been justified in calling him on it, but she did still have that attitude going on. He just couldn't believe Amanda Harrington was back at the academy and back in his class again no less. He'd had a hard enough time with her in his class last time. Not that she'd been a whiner like some of the students he'd taught over the last year and a half. He knew the academy was a shock for most students who didn't work out religiously and keep themselves in really good shape. Many whined and complained like little kids starting the first day and continuing throughout their time at the academy. Not Amanda. He remembered her having a hard time keeping up, but she'd had grit. She'd been determined and had taken everything that had been dished out with no complaints that he'd ever heard. She had definitely had something to prove. Thinking back on it, he'd known then that there was more to her than met the eye. After all, she'd survived inspector training and graduated. Now here she was back for more, within a relatively short time frame. He'd never heard of anyone advancing so quickly from inspector to special agent.

What Jake remembered about her the most was that she'd been quite the distraction. Nothing had changed there. Here he was completely distracted by her once again. He was barely even registering whom he'd checked off on the class roster since he'd looked up and seen her again. The bottom line was that there were still very few women in law enforcement compared to men, so the ratio of women to men in each class was quite low. Therefore, any female naturally stood out. However, when most guys thought of women in law enforcement they invariably pictured the butch lesbian type. Amanda Harrington was definitely the opposite of that. Not that she wasn't tough, but your first thought wouldn't be that she was in law enforcement. At first glance you might have thought more along the lines of her being a model, basically because she was so beautiful. As in eye-catchingly beautiful. She would definitely have turned his head if he'd seen her on the street. So, not only didn't she fit the stereotype, she just didn't seem like the type who would choose a career in law enforcement. Now more than ever he wondered what her story was.

"Who's the looker?" asked Donovan as they were getting ready to start the class.

"What looker?" Jake replied.

"Don't bullshit me, man. I know you know who I'm talking about," answered Donovan.

"Keep it down, we're the instructors here Don Juan." Grudgingly Jake added, "Her name's Amanda Harrington. Now put a sock in it and let's get started."

Jake had forgotten about his loud-mouthed, Don Juan impersonator and fellow instructor Larry

Donovan. As usual, he showed up right as class was supposed to start and surprise, surprise, honed in on the one attractive female in the room in less than one second flat. Well, all the instructors hadn't nick-named him Don Juan for nothing. Usually he was putting his moves on the local women in town, but who knew what he'd do with someone as attractive as Amanda right under his nose every day.

Hell was about to begin, was the thought going through Amanda's mind as the doors on each side of the front of the mat room were closed by the instructors signaling the start of class. She knew she was in much better shape than she had been a year ago and she was ready for this. At least as ready as she could be anyway. She knew what to expect this time around and she'd come more prepared. She'd worked out like a maniac and built up her stamina. She wasn't going to let anyone beat her down this time around. Not physically and not mentally. She knew she needed to have a fighter's mentality to make it through. *Bring it on!*

Jake started the class off by listing all the rules. Seemed about the same as last time. Take off your shoes upon entering any mat room, wear the required uniform, be on time, etc. So much for her little mental pep talk. She'd been ready to start sweating and now she was just standing there having to listen to a lecture.

Jake had such a presence about him, Amanda started thinking distractedly, tuning out all the rules she already knew. Maybe it was all the muscles. It could be quite intimidating. It was fun to watch all the other guys in the class trying to puff their chests out so as not to seem too puny. In reality, just about everyone looked out of shape next to the physical training instructors here at the academy. They all looked like they were in competition to become body builders. All they do is work out all day every day though, so it made sense. If only she wasn't attracted to that look, thought Amanda. OK...she had to admit it. She'd drooled over Jake a little last year already. How could she not? All those muscles outlined by the uniform polo shirt. Not to mention his tight round butt in those shorts. Yum. He was actually even better looking than she remembered. He seemed to have gotten even more muscular. He still had the military hair cut, his brown hair shorn high and tight. Some men didn't look good with super short buzz cuts, but it suited him somehow. He was also tanned a nice brown, a testament to how much time he spent outside conducting physical training every day in the summer months. Jake Marshall was one good-looking instructor.

This Donovan guy, not so much, Amanda thought as she shifted focus. Oh he had the muscles and all that going on, with bleached blond hair that reminded her of the stereotypical surfer back home in California. From a purely objective point of view she would have to say that he was attractive, but there was just something about his attitude that was almost offensive. He was one of those guys who thought he was perfect and expected everyone else to think so too. It made him very unattractive in her eyes. That's what was different about Jake. It became all the more noticeable when she compared the two of them side by side. Jake was very self-assured and just had this confidence about him. It was a quiet confidence in comparison to the outright cockiness Donovan displayed. Guess it wasn't just any guy with muscles that attracted her after all. Hmmm.

"What's your name?" yelled Donovan.

Crap. She'd been lost in thought and hadn't even noticed that everyone else was lying down on the floor mats now and she was the last one left standing. It was turning into such a wonderful day.

"Harrington," replied Amanda, knowing from last time that this was a last name only kind of environment.

"Well, Harry, how about joining the rest of us here," yelled Donovan.

"It's Harrington," Amanda answered back.

"Not anymore, Harry, and you'll end anything you address to me with a sir, per the rules that were just explained to you. Is that clear?"

"Yes sir," replied Amanda. Here we go, she thought. Back to hell with the army drill sergeants. More of the fun she'd almost forgotten about--make that tried to forget about.

Way to go Amanda, she mumbled to herself as she started the push-ups with the rest of the class. Singled out within the first five minutes of class. Stellar. Of course, being called "Harry" was a new one.

She wondered what this guy Donovan's deal was. He kept staring at her with one of those looks that usually means a guy's interested. What an idiot. Like calling her Harry was going to earn him any points.

Jake had surreptitiously been watching Amanda and had seen her turn bright red as soon as Donovan addressed her. He'd wondered what had been going on when she'd just remained standing. Leave it to Donovan to call someone out within the first few minutes of class. Each new class always started off like the proverbial deer caught in the headlights. Most didn't expect the military style of teaching, but the higher ups at the academy expected it to be run that way and it was his job to comply. So, he yelled at the students like a drill sergeant, but at the same time he tried not to be too much of an asshole. Donovan seemed to actually enjoy being the drill sergeant and was probably the reigning asshole out of all the instructors at the academy. Donovan also had this thing he did with every class where he gave certain people nicknames based on their last names. Jake could see it had gone over really well with Amanda. She'd practically had steam coming out of her ears when Donovan reiterated that "Harry" would be what she was called from now on. Don Juan definitely wasn't scoring any points there. Unfortunately, Jake was going to have to call her Harry now too. Instructors had to maintain a unified front and they'd seen the nicknames work well on problematic students. Some guys came to the academy thinking they knew everything and giving them a less than desirable nickname always seemed to take them down a peg or two. Jake had no idea what Donovan had been thinking doing it to Amanda, but little did she know that she was stuck being called Harry now for the next twelve weeks.

All Amanda could think about now was to just concentrate and keep her head down. She needed to stay below the radar and she wasn't doing a great job of that so far. This was her big chance, a whole new opportunity to advance her career. She just had to stick it out, make it to the end and graduate. No matter what. She was going to ace this criminal investigator training and earn the title of special agent that she'd always wanted. No more Inspector Harrington. It was going to be Special Agent Harrington and an in-your-face to everyone who doubted her.

To make that happen she had to remember one thing. No boys. Not this time. She didn't want to repeat the mistakes of the past. Drooling over the instructor was a bad start to the whole promise she'd made to herself. Not that getting involved with an instructor was ever going to happen, but thinking about the opposite sex in general was just a bad idea. She was here for her job and nothing else.

Keeping an eye on the clock, Amanda was glad to see that the first physical training class was almost done. She was dripping in sweat, something she really hated, and all she could think about was getting a shower as soon as possible. The instructors had really worked the class over today. The first days were the hardest, she remembered. They really tried to finish everyone off, maybe to see if anyone would just up and quit. One other classmate had received a nickname as well and she was coming to the realization that the nicknames were probably here to stay. What fun.

"Class dismissed," yelled Donovan finally.

As everyone was filing out, Amanda looked over at Jake and saw him crook his finger at her, motioning her over. "So, you got an agent slot?" asked Jake.

"That's right," answered Amanda, her heart beating double time.

"In less than a year...not bad. Congratulations."

"Thanks," answered Amanda. She didn't know why he made her so nervous, but she quickly said, "Gotta go hit the showers."

"Sure. See you later this afternoon," Jake reminded her.

Crap. As she walked away, she realized she'd completely forgotten that the physical training instructors also taught the defensive tactics classes. Two classes a day with this guy. She was doomed for sure. Well, at least she'd have some nice eye candy in class again! She turned back to see if Jake was still there and saw that he was just standing there watching her walk away. She wondered what he must think of her all covered in sweat, no make-up on, hair a mess. Why did she care? Forget about him and get a move on, she thought to herself as she headed to the women's locker room. She'd lost some valuable shower time already. It was always a rush to get cleaned up and to the next class on time. She just needed to remember to keep her head in the game.

As Amanda walked away, Jake noticed that her light brown hair had grown longer since last year and made a cute ponytail. He also thought about how she was one of the few women he'd ever come across that looked beautiful with no make-up on. She had naturally dark black eyelashes and eyebrows, which were actually quite striking up close after you got past the very expressive hazel eyes. Little emotion seemed to show on her face, and he'd rarely ever seen her smile, but those eyes of hers told a different story. It was like they changed colors right in front of him, from brown to green and somewhere in between, and telegraphed the storm that was actually brewing inside her that she was trying to keep a lid on. She also had the cutest freckles on her nose and across her cheekbones. He was a sucker for freckles. Too many women tried to cover them up with make-up and he'd never understood why. Amanda wasn't wearing a stitch of make-up, especially not after the amount of sweat the physical training class had just gotten out of each and every student, but she looked simply beautiful.

He hadn't been able to resist calling her over after class when she'd looked his way. There was just something about her. He'd noticed it last year too, but he'd been such a stickler for the rules back then that he hadn't thought too much more about it. OK...maybe a fantasy or two with her in it. Nothing beyond that though. Maybe he was just getting tired of being an instructor here at the academy. The rules didn't seem as critical anymore and he really was just flat out tired. He was coming up on his two year mark teaching here. Maybe it was time to move on. It wasn't the same anymore as it had been at the beginning. It had been an honor to be chosen to become an instructor for all the new recruits coming into federal law enforcement. He'd really reveled in it at first. Now, after all this time it just seemed like such a transient existence. You really didn't get to know anyone. Socializing with the students was frowned upon and expected to be kept at a minimum. Instructors seemed to rotate in and out on a regular basis. It was also mainly men who were instructors here. There was the occasional female instructor, but usually they were just here short term. Donovan had hooked up with some of the local females in Brunswick, the nearest city to where the academy was located here in Glynco, Georgia. That hadn't worked out so well for Jake though. The Georgian way of speaking and acting was funny in the beginning, but really wore on him now. The Georgia natives had this slow drawl, which seemed to make it take forever for them to get a sentence out. For a guy from New York like himself, it was enough to drive him crazy. He just wanted to tell them to hurry up and spit it out already. They probably thought the same about him in reverse, when compared to them he was speaking a mile a minute. Maybe he really did need to finally move on. Two years was a long time to be stuck in Glynco, Georgia. It seemed like it would be a great break from the New York Field Office he'd been working at prior to becoming an instructor. Of course, it had been great for the first few months at least. Now it just seemed kind of lonely. Ugh. He was just sounding maudlin now. He better just knock it off. Something about Amanda Harrington sure had him questioning things all of a sudden. Bad sign. He shouldn't even be thinking about her outside of class. She was just one of the many students he taught in classes all day long. There was a no fraternization rule when it came to students, faculty too actually. With faculty they most often looked the other way, as long as no problems resulted. It was different with students though. Students were definitely off limits.

Chapter 2

Finally the end of her first day back at the academy was at hand. Amanda had made it through a grueling day and was now back at her assigned barracks room just lying on the uncomfortable twin bed, staring up at the old popcorn ceiling. She was so tired she hadn't even bothered taking her uniform off yet. She just wanted to sleep right now and forget about going to get some dinner at the academy cafeteria, better known as the chow hall. Unfortunately, her brain wasn't going to cooperate with the whole sleep idea. Wanting to sleep and being able to sleep were two different things in her world. There was so much swirling around in her head about the day that she couldn't even seem to fully relax. One person definitely kept popping up in her thoughts. Jake Marshall. Defensive tactics class this afternoon with him and Donovan had been hilarious. Donovan seemed to be tripping over himself to be the one to demonstrate tactics for her specifically. He'd started the class off with some basic hand-to-hand combat moves and had chosen her to be his partner for the class demonstrations. Then he'd hovered over her and her different partners, making sure to physically correct her moves or demonstrate other options. He was a little too hands on for her already...who knew what another 12 weeks would bring.

Jake seemed to keep his distance, yet every time she'd looked up and seen him it was as if he'd been watching her. She'd been replaying their brief conversation this morning after physical training class all day. She couldn't believe that he'd pulled her aside to comment on her getting an agent slot. He'd congratulated her, sure, but he'd also mentioned how quickly she'd gotten it. She knew she had a bad habit of sometimes reading too much into things, but she really wasn't sure how to take his comments. Was he being genuine or was it one of those backhanded comments she'd gotten a lot of recently? Just because she'd moved up from being an inspector with Immigration and Customs Enforcement (ICE), to getting a shot at becoming a special agent with ICE in a short amount of time didn't mean there was anything nefarious going on. In her case it was just luck. Actually, screw luck. She'd made her own luck. She'd worked hard to put herself through college and graduated with a Bachelor of Science Degree in Criminal Justice. Her very first supervisor, when she'd come on the job as an inspector, had recognized something special in her and had encouraged her right from the beginning to become a special agent instead. Being an inspector required wearing a uniform, similar to the attire of a local beat cop. Being a special agent meant a plain clothes, undercover criminal investigator position. Both positions were federal law enforcement positions, but being a special agent had always been her wish. Starting as an inspector was just a stepping stone and her initial way in. She never thought she'd get a shot at becoming a special agent so quickly. If it hadn't been for her supervisor giving her the job announcement for the special agent position opening, she would never have applied so soon. As they say, the rest is history.

When she'd gone through the academy for inspector training, quite a few of her classmates had failed out. That meant they lost their jobs too. Every student at the academy was a probationary employee, with one of the requirements for keeping their job being that they successfully graduate from the academy. It put a tremendous amount of pressure on a person. If you didn't graduate, you were immediately terminated from your new job. It was a harsh reality and one that was bound to happen to someone again.

Now she was back for criminal investigator training and it was rumored to be much more difficult. Of course, it already seemed so much more difficult in her head because it seemed like so many people were waiting for her to fail. Last time, no one at her agency had really known her yet and hadn't really cared whether she passed or failed. The only pressure had been what she'd put on herself. This time around she had all her present and future colleagues watching and waiting. Some thought she had gotten some sort of inside deal, but she alone had to go through the numerous panel interviews, writing exams, physical fitness tests, medical exam and background investigation before finally getting this opportunity. The bottom line was that no other inspectors had even put in for the special agent job opening. They didn't have the guts. She did and she'd gotten herself a slot. The problem was that getting a slot only meant that she'd get to keep the job if she could successfully graduate from the criminal investigator training at the academy. She'd actually found out recently that it was almost unheard of for an inspector to get picked up that quickly for a special agent position. In fact, most inspectors never became special agents. One thing she had going for herself though was drive. She always wanted more for herself and didn't want to just settle. The only thing left to do now, to ensure the slot was really hers, was to graduate from the academy.

Jake was an ICE agent himself. She didn't know where he was from or what his background was, but she'd known from the beginning that he had to be under the Department of Homeland Security to be one of her main instructors. Today she had discreetly asked around and found out that they were both with the same agency. She didn't know why it had suddenly become so important to know, but him questioning her after class this morning had served as the impetus. She knew she was overly sensitive about the topic of how she got the opportunity to go from inspector to special agent so quickly. It always got under her skin when anyone asked. From recent experience it made her think that maybe Jake was once again the typical guy who thought she'd gotten the step up from inspector to special agent because she was a girl. She knew there were a lot of those guys out there. Law enforcement was still a man's world. Women were just slowly trying to break in and prove that they could do the job just as well or even better than any man. She seemed to have to prove herself over and over again and still it never seemed good enough. Oh well. She could chalk it up to daddy issues too. Having a dad that always told her she couldn't do what boys could do and that there were certain jobs just for girls in the world made her all the more determined to prove him wrong. To this day, he still frowned when she came by for a visit right after work, purposefully still wearing her uniform with her gun strapped to her hip! Just wait, as an agent she'd be required to carry her firearm 24/7. That should poleax daddy for sure!

Amanda figured she might as well get up and go to the chow hall to get something to eat. With her brain working overtime, it wasn't like she was going to get any sleep anyhow. The chow hall wasn't the greatest, but at least it was free. She didn't have a lot of money to spend like some of the other students seemed to. Of course, she also had big plans for her future, like buying a house and a new car. The bump up in pay was going to be great. She couldn't wait.

That little reminder of what the future held after graduation reenergized her. She quickly changed into shorts and a T-shirt and made the short walk across the lawn over to the chow hall. The chow hall was basically at the center of the academy. All other buildings seemed to radiate out from there. One of the benefits to the older barracks, like the one that housed the room she'd been assigned to, was that they were in close proximity to the main academy buildings. So, her room was about the length of a football field away from the chow hall. In terms of distances at the academy, that was close. So, even though she had to contend with one of the oldest barracks, at least it was in a great location.

Standing in line at the chow hall was such a drag. Amanda really wished she had a car here at the academy. That was the downside of having to travel from the west coast all the way to the east coast for the academy. Those students that lived closer drove their cars to the academy. Driving from California to Georgia had been out of the question. She didn't even have enough vacation days on the books yet to cover the time it would have taken. So, she didn't have a car to drive off academy grounds, therefore she was stuck with the food here at the academy if she wanted to eat.

She'd totally forgotten about the ogling that occurred for the first few days whenever a new female showed up at the chow hall. All the male heads turned, which meant 95 percent of the people in the cafeteria, to check out the fresh meat. It usually got a little better after everyone got a chance to check you out at least once. She figured the betting was probably already starting for sure. She'd learned that lesson already though--she wasn't the gullible fresh meat, brand new to the academy, that they thought she was. Thankfully she'd become very good at not letting it show that all this bothered her. In reality she hated it more than anything. She hated being the center of attention and being stared at was the worst. So, she calmly went through the routine of picking up a tray and getting behind the last guy in the shortest line, pretending like it all didn't faze her. Predictably the guy in front of her turned around and tried to start a conversation. She tried to answer nicely, but it was probably only a matter of time before she got the bitch label. Typically you were labeled either a flirt and then a slut, or you were a bitch. Amanda was knowingly going to choose her own label this time around. She might as well start now. No use putting off the inevitable.

Jake watched the commotion Amanda's entrance caused from a table in the corner of the chow hall. He'd been wondering when she'd show up since everyone pretty much ate at the chow hall for breakfast, lunch and dinner. Even people that had cars didn't usually drive off campus during the week. After all, the chow hall was convenient and free. As usual, a female entering the chow hall got a once over from all the guys. Being that Amanda wasn't the typical law enforcement female, she really got some major attention from everyone. The entire cafeteria had almost gone silent for a few seconds before everyone started talking again. It was funny to watch her just stride in, pick up a tray and get in line as if nothing out of the ordinary had just occurred. Of course, she'd probably experienced the same thing last year when she was here. As a matter of fact, she might be used to guys staring at her on a regular basis even in her every day life. She certainly acted like it was nothing. Watching her, Jake could tell it wasn't that she was stuck up about it though. He'd seen other females come and go at the academy that weren't half as good looking, but got a ton of attention because they were the minority. A hundred guys for every one female gave most of them a pretty big head. He could see it happen with most of them right from the beginning. Not Amanda though. Even now he could tell she was being hit on by the guys in line with her, but rather than flirting outrageously like he'd seen most other females do, she seemed more uncomfortable than anything else. Almost like she was trying to be nice, but couldn't quite manage it.

Amanda was already tired of the same drill at the chow hall every mealtime. Whoever she got in line behind seemed to think it was their lucky turn to strike up a conversation with her and it always lead up to being asked out. She was always praying for the line to speed up. Anyway, she knew the deal this time around and wasn't going to fall for any tricks. People often joked about the Las Vegas rules applying at the academy. What happens at the academy stays at the academy. She'd seen it up close and personal last time. Married guys leaving their wedding bands in their rooms and the women acting like it was a reverse harem of men at their beck and call. Promiscuous sex seemed to run rampant.

Finally it was her turn to get some food. Mystery meat, mashed potatoes, gravy, okra?...she just kept walking down the line. "I'll take a grilled cheese please," she told the cafeteria worker. Thank goodness they still had the old stand by. After getting a salad and a drink she started searching for a place to sit. It reminded her of high school days when you just hoped that someone was going to invite you to sit at their table. Luckily she quickly spotted some guys from her class and went to join them.

"Hey Harry," said Tyler Worthington III with a big wink and a smirk on his face.

"Hey Worthless," Amanda replied with an impish grin. The two of them had already commiserated with one another over the unfortunate occurrences that morning in physical training class. Some of the others at the table chuckled over their mutual greetings and considered themselves lucky to not have been given nicknames...yet.

Amanda felt herself finally beginning to relax a little and picked up her grilled cheese to take a bite. With it half way to her mouth she took a casual look around the chow hall and suddenly locked eyes with Jake Marshall. He was sitting a few tables back with some other instructors, diagonally across from her! In an attempt to act nonchalantly, Amanda went ahead and took a bite of her grilled cheese. It ended up feeling like a glob of peanut butter in her mouth. She felt like she was going to choke on it if she tried to swallow it. What was he staring at her for? Amanda finally looked away like it was no big deal and tried to ignore the fact that he was right in her line of sight. She very carefully swallowed the bite she'd taken and washed it down with a quick sip of her drink. Trying not to be obvious, Amanda quickly took another look in Jake's direction and saw that he was now engaged in conversation at his table. Maybe it had just been her mind playing tricks on her. He might have looked up right when she'd looked over and nothing more. It had seemed like they'd been transfixed on one another for longer than appropriate, but in reality it was probably mere seconds.

Jake was doing his best to keep up with the conversation the other instructors were having. Amanda had just caught him staring at her. She didn't seem surprised by it or anything, which fit his earlier thoughts on her just being used to the attention. She had stared back briefly, but had not reacted in any other way. She had taken a bite of her food and then looked away. This was all so out of the norm for him anyway. What was he doing even giving her a second thought? Yes, she was attractive. He'd seen plenty of other attractive women in his 32 years though. What was it about her that captured his attention so much this time? He studied her out of the corner of his eye. She was dressed casually in an almost shapeless outfit. That certainly hadn't grabbed his attention. In fact, she always seemed to wear clothes that were slightly too big for her. Her gym uniform was always baggy, as was her regular class uniform. She got to pick the sizes, so she was obviously doing it on purpose. It made him very curious as to why. Even with the bagginess of her clothes he could tell she had a great figure. He was so used to women flaunting what they had while they were at the academy that he did find it almost odd that she didn't. Come to think of it, most women wore the uniform a size too small! Well, from what he could see, she definitely appeared to be in better shape than her last time at the academy. It's not that her figure had changed much, but he could tell she probably worked out regularly now. He could see how well toned her arms were and her legs looked great too. She'd had a tough time keeping up with some of the running last year, he now remembered. It looked like that wasn't going to be a problem for her anymore. She was definitely one beautiful package, intriguingly wrapped. Maybe that's what had his attention this time around. The more he thought about her, the more questions he had about her. What he needed to remember though was that chip on her shoulder and he couldn't forget that attitude of hers. Suddenly Jake realized the other instructors were finished eating and were getting up to leave. He normally wolfed down his meal with the rest of them, but this time still had half of the meal left on the tray. He made a split second decision to forget about the rest of dinner and got up to leave with all the instructors.

Jake had to shake off this new obsession with Amanda Harrington. Best to just put her out of his mind. Otherwise, he'd only be asking for trouble.

Chapter 3

On her way back to her assigned barracks from the chow hall, Amanda suddenly couldn't imagine turning in for the night yet. It was barely 7 p.m. and quite frankly, her room was more like a prison cell than anything else. It was after all barely bigger than the standard eight feet by eight feet and happened to be in one of the older buildings that was all cement. So, she changed directions and headed to the gym instead. It was the same distance to the gym from the chow hall, as it was from her barracks. The three buildings were basically situated in a triangle and she had to be thankful once again that at least she'd gotten a prime location when it came to her barracks assignment.

She was hoping the gym wouldn't be too crowded and she could just lift a few weights and try and de-stress. There were always several agencies running multiple classes of law enforcement personnel through the academy all year long, so you never knew how crowded things might be. She was still feeling jet lagged from her flight from California and realized she'd probably be better off if she did go to bed right now. She knew she wouldn't be able to sleep though and this was the only thing she could think of that might settle her down.

Amanda quickly went into the women's locker room and changed into the required gym uniform of blue shorts and a light blue shirt, both with the Federal Law Enforcement Training Center insignia on them. She really hated wearing uniforms, but at least in this particular case someone else was going to be doing the washing. Storing all her stuff in her assigned locker, Amanda headed for the weight room. The gym was basically a series of long hallways with doors on either side. She'd never been in a room that had a window to the outside and luckily she remembered where the weight room was, or she'd have been wandering around trying to get her bearings. Upon entering, she quickly scanned the room for which equipment was available. It wasn't a very big room, all things considered, but luckily it wasn't too crowded and she chose the free weights to start out with. One wall of the room was floor to ceiling mirrors and she faced them, not because she wanted to watch herself, but because she'd rather not face the curious gazes of the room's other occupants. Just as she began a few simple reps, the door opened behind her and in walked Jake.

Their eyes met in the mirror and Jake's widened in surprise just as Amanda paused with the weights halfway between reps in shock. He was the last person she'd expected to see. Amanda quickly averted her gaze and almost dropped the weights in her attempt to get back on track quickly. What was it today? She couldn't seem to get away from the guy. Here she was trying to relax and he walks in? Didn't he work out enough during the day?

Jake couldn't believe Amanda was right in front of him when he walked into the gym. What was she doing here? After her first day he figured she'd be exhausted and already winding down to go to bed early. It wasn't unusual to run into students at every turn since there were only so many communal places to frequent at the academy. She just stood out more than the men. Noticing Joey Barone in the corner at the bench press confirmed it. Joey had also been at the chow hall a short time ago and was also in two of Jake's classes during the day. He wasn't shocked at seeing Joey, so why did it bother him to see Amanda here? Well, for one thing Joey had never made his pulse rate accelerate! He had to admit that Amanda did that and more.

Things were not going the way Amanda had planned at all...all day in fact. She had planned on acting like the cool, ready for anything, new recruit. No one needed to know what her real story was. Instead, she seemed to be caught off guard every time she turned around. Now, instead of this workout relaxing her, she was so amped up she probably could stand there doing nothing and her pulse rate would read as if she'd just run a six minute mile. She was simply frustrated and aggravated all at the same time. One person was to blame for that. Jake Marshall. Why she was letting him get under her skin like this she didn't know. The bottom line though was that he was the one responsible for her messed up day. She just really needed to get out of here. She needed to get away from him. The only place she knew she could accomplish that for sure was to go and lock herself in her room and just call it a day. So as not to make her departure too abrupt, Amanda started picking workout machines closer and closer to one of the exits furthest away from where Jake was. She would quickly do a set and move on. Finally the machine closest to the door was free and Amanda prepared to do her last set.

It had been about 10 minutes and Jake realized he was accomplishing exactly nothing. He'd come to the gym after dinner as he did most nights to try and get some weight lifting in. He did spend most of the day working out as part of his job, but what few people thought about was that he was repetitively doing the same routines with his classes all day and wasn't doing the workout he would choose to do if he could. In fact, most of the physical training instructors spent time after hours in the weight room. Most just seemed to do it before dinner, which is why he'd probably recently gotten in the habit of doing it after. More and more in recent months he'd just gotten tired of spending day in and day out with the same group of people. Everything had just become so repetitive that he was beginning to feel like a robot. He should probably just call it a night. The workout was supposed to help him turn his brain off from the day. Instead, he had Amanda Harrington on the brain...again. He was completely aware of her the whole time and realized he was actually counting her reps instead of his own. She seemed to be half-heartedly working out and was it his imagination or was she deliberately picking the equipment furthest from the ones he was using?

Jake grabbed his towel and headed for the door, just in time to see Amanda disappearing through it. She'd obviously decided to pull the plug too. As he came out into the hallway, he could see Amanda hurrying in the direction of the locker rooms. He wondered what her rush was all of a sudden. Someone yelled out his name and he stopped and turned as Amanda disappeared around the corner at the end of the long hallway. It was one of his students with some questions about the practical exercises that were going to be starting in the morning for his class. Most students got concerned, no matter how good they thought they were, when it came time for the actual testing of their skills. Jake reassured him as best he could and then made his way to the uniform exchange window.

Amanda hurried out of the locker room after just having changed back into the shorts and shirt she'd worn to the gym. She'd skipped the shower in the locker room in favor of taking one back at the barracks, since she was heading there right now. Even though she had to share her bathroom with the woman next door, at least she could have some privacy once she locked the connecting door. She'd changed in record time and was double checking to make sure she had all her uniform gym clothes to exchange when she walked up to the long counter in front of the uniform exchange window. She got there right as Jake Marshall was turning in his sweaty towel and waiting for a clean one. The window attendant noticed her at the window and yelled out "Size?"

Amanda called back, "Extra large shirt, large shorts," as she turned bright red in embarrassment. She always hated the way you were expected to just yell your sizes out for everyone to hear. Jake turned to her just as she was leaning over the counter to throw her soiled uniform shirt and shorts in the designated hampers. She sure had changed quickly. He noticed her blush and tried not to grin. The attendants working the uniform exchange window didn't care that they were making you yell out your clothing sizes. It was after all efficient to grab multiple sizes off the many racks of clothes for more than one person at a time, instead of coming back to the window for each individual. The attendants were used to the high volume of exchanges during the day after every class ended and they always operated as if there was a long line of students. Jake was thinking about the fact that they had exercise bras available for women too. Amanda had apparently decided to forgo using that borrowed article of clothing. Not that he could blame her. They had jock straps for guys available too, but it was one thing to have to use borrowed outer clothing and a whole other thing to choose to use borrowed intimate apparel. He imagined how red she might have gotten if she'd had to yell out her bra size too! However, she only had the very basic required uniform she was trying to exchange. He guessed she would have been embarrassed no matter what sizes she'd yelled out. It did make him think about what an enigma she was. She seemed to do the opposite of every other woman he'd ever seen come through the academy. Hearing her yelling out her gym sizes once again had Jake wondering why a woman with a knock out figure seemed to want to hide it instead of flaunt it. Many interesting layers for one very interesting woman.

"How's your first day been?" Jake asked quietly. Amanda was glad he didn't comment on her embarrassment. She'd had people laugh at her and call her out on her blushing before and she hated it. She couldn't help it when she turned red. She was easily embarrassed sometimes and as if this wasn't a complete nightmare...calling out her clothing size in front of a guy she liked.

What the hell was she even thinking? She didn't like Jake.

"It's been interesting" Amanda replied.

"How so?" Jake asked.

"How much time do you have?" Amanda half-heartedly joked.

"Plenty actually," Jake replied just as Amanda was handed clean uniform shorts and shirt. As they started walking out of the gym together Jake spontaneously said, "How about I walk you to your barracks and you tell me about it?"

Amanda just kind of fumbled with the clothes she was holding and wondered how to respond. "It's probably out of your way and I was just joking around."

"Let me walk with you anyway. I've had quite the day myself and I could use a relaxing walk. My workout tonight didn't really do the trick."

Amanda had been trying to think of a way out of the situation so it took a bit until what he said finally registered. Amanda just kind of looked at him and thought to herself that maybe she'd been too quick to judge. "So, you work out to relax?"

"Yeah, it's usually more of a stretching out of my muscles more than anything else. I usually don't get to do that kind of workout during the day so I do it at night. Most people wouldn't associate a work out with relaxation I guess."

"No, I get what you mean. I was actually trying to do the same," Amanda admitted, realizing she'd never come across anyone who understood the concept before. She quickly forgot about wanting to extricate herself from what she'd thought would be a completely awkward time together.

They both started thinking that they had something in common already.

"What barracks are you assigned to?" asked Jake.

"The one next to the gay bar," Amanda said, mentioning the one after hours place to hang out at the academy. It had been nicknamed the gay bar from way back when there were no women going through the academy. Just like the chow hall, it was a name that stuck and no one would know what you were talking about if you referred to it any other way.

"Great location, even though it is one of the older buildings," Jake commented as they continued to walk across the lawn in front of the gym.

"Yeah, you realize though that you could've been stuck walking all the way out to the furthest barracks, right?" Amanda joked, at the same time thinking she was glad she hadn't worked out too hard and gotten all sweaty, since she'd made the decision to postpone her shower. Who knew she'd end up with company on her walk back to her barracks?

"I wouldn't have minded," Jake said as he realized how true that was. He was finally unwinding a bit from the day, just enjoying her company. There was an odd sort of tension gripping him as they continued to head toward her barracks, but he had a pretty good idea what was causing it.

Amanda racked her brain for something else to say. "Do you live here at the academy?" she finally asked.

"No, I'm renting a small house on St. Simon's Island," Jake replied.

"Really? I always liked it there. The beaches are great and remind me of home. Crossing the bridge to get to the island always made me feel like I was being transported to a different world away from here." As Amanda finished saying that she realized she'd probably revealed too much in those few sentences. What had made her say all that to this man?

Jake just looked over at Amanda and thought how in tune she was with things. "What you said about crossing the bridge is exactly why I'm renting there. Other instructors here think I'm crazy for wanting to drive out there at the end of each day instead of living conveniently close."

"What is it...a 20 minute drive with hardly any traffic ever?" Amanda laughed. "That's nothing. They should try commuting where I'm from!"

Jake loved her laugh. It was a lovely low, husky sound in which he could hear her genuine amusement. And what a smile to go with it! She had nice straight white teeth and her smile lit up her whole face. He realized it was the first time he'd ever seen her really smile.

"Where is that by the way?" he asked, smiling down at her.

"Hmmm?" Amanda answered, distracted by the way he was looking at her.

"Where you're from?" Jake tried again.

"Oh...California. I'm working out of the Los Angeles Field Office," Amanda finally answered the question, quickly shaking her head, thinking the jet lag must be catching up with her.

"No kidding! A good buddy of mine's an agent there too--Mark Mitchell," Jake said, surprised by the connection.

"The firearms instructor? Sure, I know Mark."

"That also explains the statement about you loving the beach," Jake said, smiling.

"Yeah, I'm a California girl at heart," Amanda replied, smiling back.

"Really? Actually born and raised there?"

Amanda laughed and answered, "Yes, the genuine article!"

Jake was thinking again how much he really enjoyed her laugh, and the smile that came with it, and wanted to find ways to keep her laughing. He slowly realized though that they were almost at her barracks already. The time had flown and he was actually wishing now that she did have one of the barracks that was further away.

"Home sweet home away from home," said Amanda pointing to the building in front of them. The walk sure had gone quickly. She was hoping saying good night wasn't going to be awkward.

Thankfully, Jake already started stepping backwards and with a quick wave said, "Good night. See you tomorrow."

It wasn't until Amanda got to her room that she even realized she'd forgotten to put the clean gym uniform back in her locker and had been carrying it the whole time. It was also the first time since coming back to Georgia that she hadn't been complaining to herself the whole time about the horrible humidity and how sweaty and sticky she was. Wow. She must be more tired than she thought.

Chapter 4

Amanda's alarm went off bright and early the next morning. She'd set it with enough leeway to hit the snooze a few times before getting up to do the bare minimum before heading directly to the gym for physical training class. At least she had physical training first thing in the morning. What was the point in fixing herself up if she was just going to get all sweaty and have to shower again anyway? Walking out of her room into the atmospheric wall of humidity that was the quintessential Georgia summer didn't help matters either. She immediately started sweating with no effort at all. What rotten luck to be at the academy during the summer. This humidity was going to be the death of her, she thought as she half jogged to the gym. She was not a morning person and even skipping breakfast didn't give her that much added sleep time. She would take whatever time she could get though. Thankfully she'd slept like the dead after finally getting back to her room. The jet lag finally caught up to her and for once she didn't have it in her to spend time over thinking everything. Her brain was definitely kicking into overdrive now though. She wondered what it would be like to see Jake this morning. It felt like he was more than just one of her instructors after she'd spent some time with him last night. It made him seem more human somehow, more accessible. She also had to admit that in addition to her usual morning grumpiness, she'd actually had a little smile on her face since getting up and putting on her uniform gym clothes. It made her think that last night's chain of events had happened for a reason. First, she realized she could save time every morning if she didn't have to change into her gym uniform at the gym! That meant she'd gotten another round of hitting the snooze button this morning. Always a bonus! Then there was Jake Marshall...

Amanda walked into the mat room assigned to her class for that morning just as Donovan was closing the door on the opposite side. "Hey Harry," he yelled across the room. "You're just in time. Line up everybody." Jake marveled once again at how Donovan always managed to walk in right at the start of class and take charge as if everyone had just been waiting on him to give the go ahead. Jake headed in Amanda's direction to close the door she'd just come in through, glad that she was bent over taking her shoes off. He didn't know what they would have done if they'd made direct eye contact. Amanda sensed him walk by to close the door and kept herself occupied lining her shoes up with everyone else's against the wall. She knew she was turning red already and wanted to avoid any questions her face going up in flames would generate if she had any direct interaction with Jake.

Jake quickly glanced at Amanda, trying not to make it obvious, as everyone was lining up in rows of five people across and five deep. He found himself doing that way too often already, considering it was only the second day of classes. He couldn't help it though. He found himself amazed again at how beautiful she was. Even with her hair scraped back in a ponytail and her face with that clean, just splashed water on it, look. She had this natural beauty that didn't require any make-up and this morning was proof of it. She looked like she'd basically rolled out of bed and headed to class. Not many women could pull that off and still look beautiful.

Jake tried to snap himself out of this fixation he seemed to be developing for her and concentrate on the class he was supposed to be teaching. He'd spent most of last night wondering what the hell he was thinking walking a female student back to her room at night. Why was he even getting involved? The problem now was that Amanda seemed to stand out to him all that much more today, if that was even possible. Obviously spending some one on one time with her last night had already changed the usual student/instructor dynamics. Now she was already way more than just a name on the roster sheet. He knew he'd barely scratched the surface on actually getting to know her, but all he could think after last night was that he wanted to know more.

"Let's start with some jumping jacks to get you all warmed up," yelled Donovan.

"One, two..." everyone counted out loud.

"I can't hear you," yelled Donovan.

"Twenty-one, twenty-two..." Amanda continued to yell the count with the rest of the class.

Next thing you knew, they were yelling fifty-one and it didn't look like it was going to end anytime soon. Amanda started looking around and taking in the class dynamics. It was interesting how certain people always gravitated to the front of the class and others to the back. Amanda always chose to be at the back of the class. Funny how Cathy Bullough, the only other woman in the class, was always in the front row. Cathy also happened to be Amanda's suite mate back at the barracks. They didn't share a bedroom but they had to share the Jack and Jill type bathroom, which both their rooms connected to. Cathy Bullough was the typical female law enforcement type. Muscular with super short, cropped hair. Never wore make-up and dressed like a guy. She even had a deep voice that finished off her image perfectly. She seemed nice enough, but Amanda hadn't really interacted with her much. Amanda always gave the courtesy knock on the bathroom door and either heard Cathy's voice saying the bathroom was occupied or heard nothing, which meant she could go in and use it. Cathy, on the other hand, always just turned the doorknob and tried to enter. Amanda had to make a point of always remembering to immediately lock the connecting door that led to Cathy's bedroom. Too bad she wasn't in one of the newer barracks where each room had its own bathroom. Well, at least it was only two people sharing a bathroom with a toilet and shower. There were some barracks that were more like townhouses, where multiple people had to share one bathroom.

They were now in the middle of doing push ups and both Donovan and Jake were yelling at the class to keep going. Funny how she never thought of Jake by his last name. Donovan called him "Marshall" and the students just referred to him as "Sir." Amanda was dying a slow death now trying to keep up with the push-ups. She knew the drill. The instructors made them continue until the majority of the class couldn't keep up. The class was being pushed hard again today and they were only 20 minutes into the hour long class.

"Let's head outside for a run, people," Donovan announced.

"Do we have to?" Amanda heard someone say.

Then she saw Donovan point at whom she assumed was the culprit and immediately yell back, "Last name?"

"Bullough," came the reply. Uh oh, thought Amanda. Bad move on Cathy's part.

"OK, Bulldog, you're leading the pack today. Let's go!" yelled Donovan.

Another nickname born.

"Everyone line up in two rows," yelled Jake once they got outside the gym.

They started off at a slow pace, marching down the road. Jake started yelling, "Left. Left. Left, right, left."

Then Donovan piped in with, "I can't hear you." It seemed to be his favorite line, after which everyone started yelling along with the cadence. It was all once again just like out of a movie about the military. Then the marching turned into a slow jog and then the speed really picked up. Amanda hated running. It was her least favorite form of exercise and here they were on day two with the instructors already putting the hurt on. She remembered some of the runs from last time she was here where they had the academy's very own ambulance and crew following just in case they had people falling out of formation. No joke.

Amanda turned to look back to see if they were being followed by the ambulance on this run. No sign of them. That meant they were probably only going to run a few miles. Just as Amanda turned back with a sigh of relief, she stumbled into Worthless who'd been jogging in front of her.

"Sorry," they both said to each other at the same time. Worthless had a shoelace that had come undone and Amanda hadn't been paying attention when he'd stumbled, so she'd knocked them both out of formation.

"Harry!" yelled Jake. "Fall back, drop and give me ten push-ups. Worthless, tie your shoe and get back in formation."

Amanda went to the back of the line of runners and dropped to the ground to do the ten push-ups. She was so pissed at Jake she found herself cursing under her breath the whole time. By the time she was done with the push-ups she was so out of breath that she could barely get the curses out. Meanwhile, she could hear Donovan yelling in the distance, ridiculing Worthless for not knowing how to tie his shoe properly.

"Catch up to the rest of the pack and get back into formation," yelled Jake from up ahead as she got up after push-up number ten.

The jerk then started jogging right next to her as she was desperately trying to catch up with the rest of the class who had kept on running when she'd had to stop and do her push-ups. Her legs hurt so bad now and it was everything in her to catch up.

"Nice of you to join us again," yelled Donovan as Amanda made it back to the end of the line. She saw Donovan signal for Jake to switch places with him. As Jake sped up to get to the front of the formation, Donovan added, "Maybe you'll pay more attention in the future." She was really starting to hate him.

Amanda also started thinking that having the ambulance following on every run wouldn't be such a bad thing after all.

Things pretty much continued down hill after that. The run seemed to go on and on. Other people got called out to do push-ups and had to catch up to the back of the line. She knew how things worked, but did she have to be the first one to get called out? And by Jake? Amanda was pissed off the whole rest of the run at how Jake had used that stupid nickname to yell at her. If anything, the anger kept her going though. Cathy had already been called out for push-ups for slowing down at the front of the line, along with several others. It was going to be a long day. She was beginning to wonder if it was her imagination or if the instructors were pushing the agents a lot harder than they'd ever pushed the inspector classes. She had thought she was in much better shape this time around, but she was wiped out once again.

They were all a sorry looking bunch when the class run finally ended back at the gym. Amanda's shirt was soaked with sweat and her shorts were sticking to her legs. Yuck. Her hair was also plastered to her head and her ponytail had sagged a long time ago. Donovan dismissed the class in front of the gym so everyone could head to the locker rooms. That's when Amanda finally noticed that not all of her classmates had made it to the gym yet. There were students back on the road, in the distance, who hadn't been able to keep up. They'd been left behind to walk back. Amanda was familiar with that experience. That had been her the last time around. Guess she'd made some improvements after all.

"Sorry about the push-ups today Harry," Worthless said as he came up alongside her on their way down the hallway.

"No worries Worthless," Amanda said back, thinking distractedly about how their nicknames weren't a big deal between the two of them. If anything, they both found them amusing. So why had her nickname mattered so much when it came from Jake?

Amanda jerked herself back to the present and continued saying, "I wasn't paying attention, so it was my own fault." The whole nickname thing was something to ponder at a later time.

"Well, I still got chewed out for not having my shoe tied properly!" Worthless joked.

"Yeah you did. I couldn't help but hear Donovan yelling at you. At least you got to skip the push-ups though," Amanda said back.

"That's only because the instructors knew I probably wouldn't be able to tie my shoe, do push-ups and ever be able to catch up with the class again at the pace they had us going!" Worthless said, laughing at himself.

"No joke. They smoked us pretty good today, didn't they." Amanda said tiredly.

"It's all part of the game. Hang in there Harry! I'll catch you later," Worthless said as he headed to the men's locker room and she continued on to the women's side.

The rest of the morning schedule involved a couple legal classes before it was time for lunch at the chow hall. Then the afternoon was comprised of what she liked to call the "what not to do" classes.

They always had lawyers as the guest speakers for these classes and they droned on and on about ethics and how to behave once you had a badge and gun. There was always a lot of legal jargon that was a real snooze. It all seemed like common sense to Amanda, but looking around she realized that the people who probably should be listening carefully were asleep at their desks. That's what pretty much happened in the classes where you weren't going to be tested on the material. There was always someone in the class who asked at the beginning of every class if the material presented was going to show up on a test. If the answer was no, no matter how much the person might still insist on the importance of the material, the majority of the class tuned it out. That's probably why there was a test on most of the material presented. Looking around, it was amusing to see the different techniques for sleeping in class while appearing to still be awake. She'd never mastered it, so the paper in front of her just became filled with doodling.

Time for defensive tactics next. The second to last class of the day. At least changing into gym clothes wasn't required even though the classes were also taught in the mat rooms at the gym. Was it really only day two?

Amanda knew the first week was one of the hardest. For her, it was particularly difficult to get back into the routine of things again. Nothing was new to her this time around, so it seemed all the more monotonous already. Plus, the academy was very taxing, both mentally and physically. No matter

who you were, the long days were going to take a
toll. She also knew jet lag was still playing a roll
too. Once that was behind her though, she knew
things would get a little better. The days would start
to mesh together and in the middle of the twelve
weeks it would seem like it would never end, but at
the end it would seem like it just sped by. From
experience, she knew she better enjoy some of the
down time this week, because once the testing started
it was a whole other kind of stress.

Chapter 5

It was finally time to blow off some steam. Thursday night had arrived and seeing as how the week was almost over, what could it hurt to join some classmates at the only bar at the academy. The gay bar was the only communal place to hang out after hours on academy grounds and even though it was usually full of just a bunch of guys, Amanda knew from last time around that it could be fun for a few hours if the drinking stayed under control.

Amanda walked in and saw Worthless straight away. He waved her over to the table where he was sitting with some of the other guys from class.

"Glad you could make it Harry," Worthless said with a smile.

"Thanks Worthless. What are you drinking?" answered Amanda, sitting down at the table.

"Beer of course," answered Worthless. "Us southern boys don't go for any of those fancy drinks, ya know!" Worthless gave her an exaggerated wink and Amanda laughed.

Someone from their table chimed in with, "Aren't you Worthless the third or something? You are hardly a redneck, more like southern aristocracy."

"I'm drinking a beer though, aren't I?" Worthless responded cheekily, dismissing the topic quickly.

She really liked Worthless a lot but, damn it all, thanks to their stupid nicknames she realized that she didn't even know his real name! Obviously it was a touchy subject anyway. She'd noticed the quick grimace before his glib response. Oh well, what started out as a joke after classes, with everyone using their given nicknames with each other, had somehow stuck and just become the norm. All the guys from class that she seemed to be hanging out with regularly had gotten a nickname already. She didn't know what that said about the company she was keeping. However, everyone probably didn't think of her as other than Harry anymore either!

Amanda headed to the bar to get her own drink. How funny that the gay bar was even called a bar. It was more like a big former cafeteria with sterile walls and laminate floors. It even had the same tables and chairs you would expect to see in an industrial type cafeteria. Sure, there was a decent size, U-shaped counter that acted as a bar. It was like one of those old counters you'd see at a truck rest stop in the middle of nowhere. The bar area, in theory, could be separated from the main room by these ugly old accordion style doors. She'd never seen them closed before and wondered if someone had just never bothered to remove them. Looking around she realized that not a single thing had changed. There was still nothing decorating the walls and the place looked as devoid of decor as it always had. There was still the karaoke machine sitting in the corner of the main room. Just looking at it made her shudder. The few times she'd seen it in use the last time she'd been at the academy had been late into the evening when most people were way past their limit. It hadn't been pretty. Her new goal was to leave the bar before anyone even thought of giving the karaoke machine a second look.

Back at the table, her classmates were replaying some of the highlights of the week. "Hey Harry, how'd you like doing sit ups attached to the instructor?" was yelled by someone further down the table. Everyone started laughing, chiming in their two cents.

"Just another day in hell, boys." Amanda answered flippantly. That set them off on another round of laughter before they went on to the next topic. One thing she'd learned from her time working in law enforcement was how to fit in with the boys. She could now banter back and forth with the best of them.

What she didn't need was a reminder of the other morning during physical training.

Every once in a while the instructors took the class outside instead of doing the usual stuff in the mat room. This particular morning it was sit-ups in the damp grass. Pure joy. The class had to form two lines facing each other. Then everyone was instructed to link elbows with the person on either side of them and then sit down. Next you had to hook legs with the person across from you. This was all supposed to give stability for the sit-ups. Amanda had purposefully ended up on the outside of one side, so she only had to link elbows with one other person. What she didn't realize was how lopsided it was going to make doing the sit ups. She seemed to have one arm flailing about while the rest of her body was being pulled at an odd angle by the other two guys she was attached to.

They were on the fifth sit-up when the next thing she knew, Jake was sitting down next to her. Before she could think about what he was up to he'd linked elbows with her and was joining in on the sit-ups! He didn't say a word, just seamlessly blended right in and continued counting with the rest of the class. The sit-ups were a breeze after that. Despite how peeved she still was at him, Amanda couldn't help but admire all those muscles up close. He was pulling her up next to him like she weighed nothing. His arm was triple the size of hers and she just kept watching the flex of his muscles out of the corner of her eye. This was one exercise she for once wouldn't have minded continuing!

They'd done 200 sit-ups as a class. The weak were pulled up by those that were stronger. Normally she would have hated the invasion of her personal space, but she had to admit to herself that she'd been solely focused on where she and Jake couldn't help but touch the whole time. Of necessity he'd been close enough that their legs had touched from ankle to thigh and their arms had of course been linked. Every up and down motion had rubbed their bare skin against one another. She had to admit there was definitely a certain chemistry with Jake that she could not ignore. She remembered how she'd tried not to rub against the guy on the other side of her, but with Jake it was all good. Thinking back on it, she once again had to admire how he'd done the sit ups with no one across from him, pulling her along, and in the end hadn't even seemed winded.

She hadn't needed anyone bringing it up again because it hadn't been far removed from her thoughts since it happened.

Amanda finally realized she'd been lost in thought for a while and hadn't really been listening to the conversations around her, nor had she been participating much at all. Not that anyone had noticed, obviously. Sure, Worthless being the major flirt that he was, had made a few comments to her here and there, but nothing a few vague replies hadn't tempered. He was tall, dark and handsome and basically a really nice guy. There'd even been some talk about him being a great catch--coming from a wealthy, well respected family. Yet here she was sitting next to him, thinking about Jake.

She glanced at her watch and saw that it was starting to get closer to the possible karaoke hour. She quickly finished the one beer she'd been nursing the whole night and got up to leave. She made it seem like she was just going to the bathroom to avoid any crap from the guys. She didn't need the comments on how she was such a lightweight and the questions on why she couldn't stay longer. She remembered all the pressure from last time where everyone tried to drink each other under the table. Talk about learning from her mistakes! So, instead of making a left into the women's bathroom she just kept walking and headed right out the front door of the bar. Breathing in the fresh air, although still humid as ever, felt good. What a week it had already been so far.

"Hey!" she heard someone call out behind her when she was already on the path heading away from the back of the building. Amanda turned around to see Jake jogging to catch up with her.

"What's up?" she asked, deliberately trying not to make eye contact. She was so surprised to see him, especially after what she'd just been thinking about at the bar. She was sure she was turning bright red.

"Why are you heading out so early?" Jake asked.

"Not you too?" Amanda said with a grimace on her face.

"What's that supposed to mean?" Jake said, looking puzzled.

"Never mind. I didn't even know you were inside. Some of the instructors getting together tonight?" Amanda asked, knowing that was the only time she'd ever seen instructors at the gay bar.

"Yeah, a last minute meeting of sorts," Jake answered.

"What's up?" Amanda asked again, not really wanting to talk to him. He was already on her mind way too much given the rules she'd set for herself this time around at the academy.

"Just wanted to see how you were doing," Jake said, wondering about the vibe he was picking up on.

"I'm tired. Heading back to my barracks," Amanda answered curtly, hoping he'd take the hint as she turned to start walking down the path again. She was trying to remind herself that he was an instructor and not a student. They shouldn't even be talking to one another like this. Besides, she was still kind of upset about him calling her Harry the other day. She knew it was irrational to hate that stupid nickname so much coming from him, but not think anything of it coming from her classmates. She wished she hadn't even given it a second thought.

"You seem kind of down. Everything OK?" Jake asked as he fell into step beside her. He'd been watching her sitting, seemingly lost in thought, at the table with her classmates. He'd become preoccupied himself after seeing her there, hardly paying attention to what was going on at his own table. That wasn't surprising, since he'd been thinking about her almost nonstop since the sit-ups in the grass yesterday. He'd acted on impulse when he'd seen her struggling to do the sit-ups with no one to anchor her on one side. Being that close to her with their bodies rubbing together all along one side had been quite the experience. He couldn't remember ever being that turned on by someone, while doing something that mundane. Actually, he couldn't remember the last time he was that turned on by anyone...period.

"It's just been a rough first week," Amanda answered, trying to cut him some slack. He didn't deserve this attitude from her.

"Yeah, it takes some getting used to, being back here, doesn't it?" Jake answered, wondering what was going on. Something seemed off.

"You don't know the half of it," Amanda said quietly, just looking ahead as she continued walking along.

"So, tell me about it," Jake said, hoping she'd clue him in.

"I don't think so. Like I said, I'm tired and I just want to get back to my room," Amanda said, knowing that being alone with him like this was a mistake. Every interaction with him seemed to put him in her thoughts even more. It made it all the more difficult for her to think of him as one of her instructors and nothing more.

Jake knew he should just let her go. He was an instructor and she was a student. Instead he found himself saying, "I'll walk with you," rationalizing it by thinking he just wanted to spend a little time with her. What was the harm in that? He knew it wasn't the best idea, but he couldn't seem to stop himself from wanting to. He also had to admit that he'd felt the immediate sexual tension arcing between them from the moment he'd caught up with her on the path, knowing it was a forbidden thing yet unable to resist the lure of it.

Once she realized he was going to walk her back to her barracks, Amanda started picking up the pace a little. She'd felt the same electric charge in the air and was finding it more difficult to ignore the longer they were in proximity to one another.

Jake touched her arm lightly and said, "Hey, wait up. What is up with you? I thought we could chat a little about how things have been going for you. I'm trying to be nice here."

"Nice?" Amanda stopped and sputtered, irritated by the zing that had just gone up her arm at his touch. Why did he, of all guys, have the ability to affect her this way?

Turning to face him Amanda said, "Oh really. Just like you were being nice when you called me out the other day on the fun run?" At this point she thought starting an argument might change the vibe in the air.

"That's what this is about?" Jake asked, seeing the spark of anger in her eyes as she looked up at him. She was so beautiful, she took his breath away.

"No. Just forget it. I really am just tired," she said wearily and turned to go. She was being ridiculous now and she hated that she'd even brought it up. Why couldn't she handle Jake the way she did the other guys?

Jake couldn't let her leave like that. He knew she was trying to fight the attraction between them. They could both feel it and the temptation to act on it was too great to resist.

"Mandy!"

She turned back in surprise and Jake just grabbed her face with both hands and kissed her. Right there on the path between the gay bar and her barracks. At first she was too stunned to react. She was almost frozen in place. Then the warmth of his hands and lips on her face registered and her lips softened and parted. His lips on hers were amazing. She loved the feel of his big hands cradling her face and she felt herself go up on her tippy toes so she could wrap her arms around his neck. She felt like she was in a dream sequence. The way he'd just grabbed and kissed her made her feel like she'd finally met a man, not just a boy. This was a man who knew what he was doing.

Jake couldn't believe it. He was finally kissing her and it was better than he could've imagined. Her lips were so soft and after her initial shock seemed to yield to him right away, as if she wanted this kiss as much as he did.

"Say it again," Amanda murmured.

"What's that?" Jake mumbled in reply, all the while kissing her cheeks and then starting down her neck.

"My name. Say my name again the way you just said it."

"Mandy," Jake said softly and took her lips again in a steamy kiss.

She could feel herself melting on the inside. She'd never heard her name said more sweetly. It seemed like he was telling her, just with the inflection in his voice, that he cared about her. It also happened to be her favorite shortening of her name.

Jake pulled her off the lit path and resumed kissing her in the shadows cast by the trees. His arms were wrapped around her now, holding her close. She loved the feel of those muscled arms surrounding her.

"You know, I wasn't even sure you knew my real name," Amanda said quietly.

"Of course I know your name."

"Then why did you call me Harry the other day in class?" Amanda couldn't help but ask.

"Is that why you've been upset?" he said, looking deeply into her eyes.

"Maybe," Amanda said, breaking eye contact self-consciously.

"I've got to call you Harry just like Donovan does, don't you see that? I can't treat you any differently in class. I've got to be the instructor and you've got to be like any other student," Jake said earnestly.

"I guess you're right," Amanda grumbled in response.

"You know I'm right. Don't you realize that I have to follow Donovan's lead when he throws out those crazy nicknames for everybody? We're supposed to work as a team and it's all part of the military mindset here. Donovan's a new instructor and his philosophy is that the nicknames are a form of motivation. It was originally intended to take the cocky guys down a notch or two, but he's gotten so carried away now that he's nicknaming everyone that stands out in any way. You can't take it personally Amanda. OK?"

"Stick with Mandy. It's one of my favorite nicknames," she said, smiling up at him with that beautiful smile of hers that lit up her whole face.

"Oh Mandy. You're something else, you know that?"

It could be dangerous if he ever found out just how much she loved it when he said her name that way. She might have given him a clue when she reached out and pulled his head back down to hers for another kiss. Being that bold was completely out of the norm for her, but she just couldn't help herself. Jake seemed to bring things out in her that even she was surprised by. It was well worth it though because the pay off was like nothing she'd ever experienced before.

Bliss. Kissing Jake was bliss. Her heart was pounding and she felt more alive than ever before. It was like the purest shot of adrenaline ever.

Jake was feeling the same way. He felt like he couldn't get enough of kissing Amanda. There was almost an innocence about her, but then when she reached up and initiated the kiss he caught a glimpse of this other side of her that really intrigued him. He wanted to explore that side of her and more. He felt himself wanting to know everything there was to know about her. His heart felt like it was beating strongly again for the first time in ages. He could almost feel his blood coursing through his veins. He really just wanted to carry her off like a caveman and have his way with her! He knew he needed to ease back on showing how hungry he was for her though. He couldn't believe they were right outside where anyone could see them. Thankfully there weren't any other people leaving the bar this early. If they were caught by anyone there would be serious repercussions. Jake couldn't believe the sudden turn of events. It had all been completely spontaneous! He was on such a high at the moment. He didn't even want to consider the possible ramifications of his actions right then.

Jake finally took Amanda's hand and started walking her back toward her barracks. They were both silent, almost lost in their own world, happy just to be with each other.

Jake stopped in the shadows of a big willow tree across the parking lot from the stairs up to her room. He took her face in his hands again and kissed her softly. "Get some sleep. I'll see you tomorrow."

Amanda mumbled a good night and felt like she was sleep walking the whole way to her room. What had just happened? She couldn't even fathom it yet. As she got to the open hallway connecting all the rooms on the second floor and was standing in front of the door to her room, she turned to look back toward the trees and saw Jake wave and disappear into the dark.

Chapter 6

What had she been thinking last night? Amanda was wondering on her way to the gym the next morning. She felt weird about having kissed an instructor...and not just any instructor at the academy, but the one she had to see for two classes a day every day. All she could think about as she was trudging along was that it could end up being so awkward. She couldn't believe all that had happened already and it was only week one! She hated these typical morning after thoughts. Why couldn't she think about these things before they happened? Then keep them from happening? Of course, when she thought about their very first kiss last night and how perfect it had been, she went from kicking herself to daydreaming about it happening again. It was going to be a very long day.

Amanda was very worried that she was falling into the same trap of the past. She didn't want to repeat the mistakes she'd made the last time she was here at the academy. What happened to her vow of no boys this time around? Of course, Jake was hardly a boy. He was definitely a man.

Her two classes today with Jake as the instructor were really taking their toll on her emotions. She would psych herself up thinking she could stop herself from getting involved past this point and then all he had to do was glance at her in class and she started blushing. So much for her attempt at being calm, cool and collected. This first week of classes had been quite the roller coaster ride and she knew she needed to lie low to give herself a chance to sort it all out. Good thing she already had something bland planned for tonight. There was one valuable thing she'd learned her last time at the academy...

Friday night was the perfect time to do laundry. Amanda knew not everyone thought that, but that's what she was counting on. When the laundry rooms got crowded it became chaos. She was trying to avoid that by doing her laundry on the night most students made plans to leave the academy grounds as soon as possible. Trial and error had made her stumble on the solution to at least one problem last time around. Amanda left her room and went across the parking lot to the laundry facility for her building. She'd already put two loads of laundry in washing machines and was going back to put them in the dryer.

"What do you think you're doing?" Amanda said as soon as she walked into the laundry room and spotted some guy in the process of taking her first load of laundry out of the washing machine.

"Your laundry was done," came the disgruntled reply.

"It couldn't have been done for more than a minute. How about having the decency to give a person a chance to unload it?" Amanda said in a huff. So much for not having these issues on a Friday night.

"Listen, we all need to do laundry around here and most people don't empty the washers or dryers when they're done. They just leave their clothes as if these appliances are their own personal ones. So, your clothes get taken out and stacked somewhere so the next person can get theirs done," this guy says.

"I know the deal, but I swear that machine just finished and you didn't even give it a few seconds before you started unloading it. I even had a timer set to avoid my underwear being on display, thank you very much," Amanda said with her voice increasing an octave.

"What's the big deal anyway. You don't want anyone seeing your thong underwear?" The guy had the gall to laugh as he held one up!

Amanda felt herself turn beet red, which also happened to be the color of the thong being held up. She was now not only embarrassed but also super angry. She was just about to lunge at the guy when in walked Jake Marshall.

"Is there a problem here?" asked Jake, looking back and forth between Amanda and the guy he had walked in on her arguing with.

"No," answered Amanda with her teeth clenched as she swiped her underwear out of the guy's hand and attempted to gather up all her wet clothes.

"Let me get a dryer open for you," said Jake, having quickly taken in the situation.

"I don't need any help," answered Amanda as she attempted to open the dryer door with her arms full.

Jake shrugged and just leaned a hip against a washing machine, crossing one foot in front of the other, watching as Amanda struggled to do it on her own.

"What, you've got nothing better to do than stare at me?" Amanda said irritatedly to Jake.

"Not really. I'm just waiting for a washing machine to free up," Jake answered with a grin. "Besides, I'm not your enemy...I just got here to do some laundry," Jake said with his hands in the air, giving the universal sign of "don't shoot" or "I surrender."

"You're right. He's my enemy right now," Amanda said, angrily pointing to the guy she'd been arguing with.

"What agency are you here with?" Jake asked the laundry culprit.

"Border Patrol," came the reply just as the guy was putting in his coins to start the washing machine.

"Figures," Amanda said under her breath. Then she turned to the guy and said, "Let me guess, you've got at least another four months to go here at the academy, right?"

"Actually five, since I've only been here a month so far," he replied with an extra big grin, knowing she was hoping he might be finishing the academy soon. "I'll see you around!" was his parting shot as he exited the room.

"Damn border patrol agents," Amanda mumbled to herself as she turned on the dryer. She took a quick peek over her shoulder and of course, Jake was still in the same spot. He'd probably heard her mumblings if the stupid grin on his face was anything to go by.

"You know those guys think they run the place just because their time at the academy is the longest," Amanda said, trying to hide her red face by not turning to look at Jake again. This whole situation was so embarrassing.

Jake simply said, "No comment."

"What are you doing here anyway?" Amanda finally spun around and asked Jake.

"I already told you. Laundry." Jake said with his arms crossed and his hip still leaned up against one of the washing machines. Amanda was trying really hard to ignore the sexy pose.

"Why here?" Amanda asked.

"Instructors are allowed to do their laundry at any of the facilities here at the academy," Jake replied as if reading from a rule book.

"I get that. You still haven't answered the question though. Why here? Why this laundry facility when there are several other ones to choose from?" Amanda said with squinted eyes, just daring Jake to say what she already knew.

"Why not?" was Jake's nonchalant reply as he turned toward a washer that had just finished its cycle.

Amanda stomped out of the laundry room and down the hall to the small TV room where you could hang out until your laundry was done. Obviously she was going to have to stay and be on hand right when her laundry finished. She'd seen people's laundry stacked on top of washers before, but it had never happened to her. Guess it wasn't as big a deal for the guys to have their laundry messed with, but when you're one of the few women doing laundry it changes things. The last thing she needed was her underwear on display again.

"What's on?" Jake asked as he walked into the TV room. Amanda hadn't even been paying attention so she had no idea. One of the two other guys present answered as Jake took a seat on the couch. Thankfully Amanda was sitting in one of the two available overstuffed chairs in the room when Jake came in. There was limited seating available on a good day. Four people could sit comfortably, with two on the couch and one in each of the chairs positioned on either side of the couch. Anything beyond that got quite cozy and she'd seen the room filled with folding chairs on sports game nights.

Amanda should have known Jake's next stop would be the TV room too. After all, he didn't have a room here at the barracks. She was still fuming over the embarrassing incident with her laundry though, so she hadn't been thinking clearly.

"This show is just about over, isn't it? What's on next?" Jake asked the two guys.

Amanda decided to slip out the door as they were talking to go and check on her other load of laundry. She knew she'd started the washers about ten minutes apart. The laundry room hadn't been as empty as she'd expected for a Friday night and as much as she hated to admit it, she knew the border patrol guy had been right. There were obviously a lot more machines full of laundry than there were people around. She just wished he hadn't chosen her machine to be the one to empty.

"Leaving so soon?" Jake asked as he came into the laundry room a few minutes later. "Your laundry can't possibly be dry yet."

"True," Amanda responded. "But I have a second load in a washing machine that should be just about done and I don't want a repeat of the earlier incident."

"How about coming back when you're done to watch a movie with me?" Jake asked, knowing she was probably planning to head back to her room at the barracks instead of to the TV room again.

"I doubt those guys in there will want to watch a movie." Amanda replied with a knowing smirk.

"I'll get rid of them and we'll have the place to ourselves," Jake said, once again leaning nonchalantly against a washing machine in that sexy pose that Amanda was becoming more and more distracted by.

"How do you think you're going to manage that?" Amanda asked. "You can't just kick them out."

"It won't be a problem. But, seriously, it's Friday night and we're both here doing laundry, so let's make the most of it and watch a movie together. What do you say?" Jake asked with this little boy pleading look on his face.

That look, combined with the sexy pose, was definitely hard to resist. Amanda just stood there thinking to herself how cute he looked just waiting patiently for her answer. That's one thing she really liked about Jake. He never really pressured her and always just seemed relaxed and quietly confident about life in general.

"If you can get those guys to agree, then I'll consider it." Amanda answered, thinking there was no way they were all going to want to watch the same movie, if they even agreed to a movie in the first place.

"OK. Meet me back in the TV room when you're done here." Jake said and sauntered off.

Amanda wondered at the irony of life as she was pulling her wet clothes out of the washing machine. She had decided to do her laundry on Friday night to avoid any kind of social entanglements and what happened? She ended up around the very guy she was trying to avoid. So, she was finally being honest with herself. She was trying to avoid Jake. He did things to her equilibrium that she didn't want to deal with. She kept wanting to play by the rules she'd set for herself here at the academy, but it was harder than she ever thought it would be. Jake made it harder than she ever would have expected. Oh well. It was Friday night and she would have just been spending a depressing evening in her room after doing laundry. It might be fun to see the outcome of things in the TV room!

"Pick which one you want to watch," was the first thing Jake said as Amanda walked into the TV room.

"Where'd the guys go?" Amanda asked in bewilderment. She'd seen in the past how possessive people got over the TV room and the rule was that the first one there controlled the remote.

"They left after the show was over," Jake replied with a chuckle.

"So you knew all along that you wouldn't have to convince them of anything?" Amanda said, looking at him suspiciously.

"Yes. My only concern was that someone else might come in and start watching something while I was in the laundry room with you!" Jake answered, still chuckling.

"You sneak!" Amanda said accusingly, laughing herself now.

"Well, if you'd stuck around a minute longer, you would have heard them yourself saying that they had plans later tonight and that the TV would be ours shortly. Plus, you can see this place is starting to get pretty deserted. Most people don't think of doing laundry on Friday nights. They think of getting away from the academy as quickly as possible for a while," Jake said.

"That's why I'm doing laundry tonight," they both said almost simultaneously and had to just laugh together.

"Guess we both think alike," Jake responded.

"At least when it comes to the best night to do laundry anyway," Amanda responded in an attempt to halt the banter and stop herself from getting sucked in by his charm.

"Well, let's see about movies then. Pick one." Jake said again, holding up about five different movie choices.

Surprisingly there was one movie that Amanda had actually been wanting to see anyway, so the choice was easy. She thought to herself how all five of the movies Jake had chosen had similar themes. There was just enough violence to keep him interested and a romance between the main characters thrown in to keep her interested. Obviously they did think alike on movies too. She wasn't going to admit any of this to him though.

Jake got some popcorn ready as well, thanks to the vending machines in the hallway and the microwave setup. So, they both sat on the couch this time to eat popcorn and watch the movie. Amanda had her head leaned back on the couch and looked over at Jake just as the movie began. He sensed her watching him and turned his head to give her a smile. He had a great smile. Nice straight white teeth and those great lips. She caught herself before going too far along that train of thought. She wondered to herself how slick he really was in this department. He'd gotten her on the couch with him, watching a movie together after she'd been sure that she would be going back to her room shortly. Oh well. She figured she might as well try and enjoy herself. It had been a hell of a week and this might be just what she needed to relax.

Jake started to relax after a short time too, once he realized Amanda was going to stay and wasn't going to come up with an excuse to ditch him. He hadn't been sure at first what her reaction would be. He knew she'd been expecting the two guys to still be watching TV when she'd walked in, but she'd actually been a good sport about it all. When she let her guard down, she was really fun to be around. He really loved her laugh and had gotten a kick out of her basically laughing at herself and the situation when she'd called him a sneak. It proved that his instincts about her were right and he wasn't wasting his time getting to know her. So, he put his feet up on the small coffee table in front of the couch and settled in.

It was fun watching the movie together, Amanda thought. They laughed at the same parts and it was just a companionable way to spend a Friday night. Maybe they could end up just being good friends. So what if their hands occasionally touched on the way into the popcorn bag? He didn't seem fazed by it. She, on the other hand, kept getting a little zing up her arm. She was actually becoming increasingly distracted, trying to time the reach for popcorn a little better so there would be no touching. She finally had to admit to herself, once and for all, that there was an undeniable chemistry with Jake that couldn't be ignored, no matter how hard she might try. It was there between them every time they were in the same room together. This was one guy she obviously couldn't just be friends with.

Jake knew exactly what Amanda's dilemma was. Good thing he'd seen the movie before because he was barely paying attention after a while. There was this tension between them whenever their hands inadvertently touched. He knew the popcorn had been a great idea. He was trying not to show any reaction because he didn't want Amanda deciding not to stick around. So, he kept trying to be nonchalant about their hands touching, all the while knowing she was trying to keep it from happening. This Friday night was shaping up much better than he could have imagined.

About halfway through the movie they took a short break and made sure all their laundry had been moved to the dryers. It wasn't too much longer after that before Jake just gave up all pretense of even watching the movie anymore. He finally just turned his head sideways and looked over at Amanda. They were both kind of slouched on the couch by now and he just admired how pretty she looked. She was wearing sweatpants and a T-shirt, with her hair loose around her shoulders and her feet tucked up Indian style. She had no make-up on that he could see and she just looked simply beautiful. He once again thought to himself how he couldn't remember the last time he'd seen a woman with no make-up on that looked this naturally beautiful.

Amanda knew he was looking at her, but was trying to pretend she didn't. She kept telling herself to just watch the movie. Finally she just said, "What?"

"What?" Jake said back, trying not to grin.

Amanda turned to look at him and he said, "You're beautiful."

Amanda was stunned for a moment and then tried to blow off the comment by saying, "Yeah, right. I'm sitting here in sweats after a long day running around this academy and you tell me that? What kind of line are you trying to feed me here?"

"No line. You're beautiful. It's a compliment."

Just as Amanda was going to say something else, Jake put a finger over her lips and leaned in to replace his finger with his lips. Amanda just kind of sighed into his mouth as they kissed. She'd be lying to herself if she said she hadn't wanted him to kiss her again. She'd just been planning on avoiding a situation where it could occur again. So much for that plan.

He pulled her closer on the couch as the kiss became more heated. She put her hands out in front of her and encountered his chest. At first her hands kind of fluttered like a butterfly, like she didn't really know what to do with them, then they just landed on his chest and decided to stay put. Wow. What a chest. She was finally getting to feel all those muscles she'd admired from afar. Her hands moved over his pecs and she let out this hum of approval. Jake was quite enjoying it as well. He could tell she'd been unsure when he'd first kissed her again, but now she was moving her hands over his upper chest and by the sound of her little hums, she was enjoying exploring. Jake was holding back because he realized they were in a public area and even though the building seemed deserted, anyone could walk in on them at any time. The distant buzzing of a dryer timer finally made Amanda think about where they were as well.

"I better go check on my laundry," Amanda said quickly.

"I'll come with you," said Jake, turning off the TV.

After collecting all their clean laundry Amanda was prepared to part ways.

"Let me help you up to your room with that," Jake said. "I'll just put my clothes in my car and be back in a minute."

Before Amanda could even respond, Jake was out the door to the parking lot. She was thankful she had two laundry bags to put her clothes in when Jake returned and took one from her. They headed out across the practically empty parking lot to the stairwell with the most direct access to her second floor room. Amanda was becoming increasingly nervous the closer they got to her room and silence reigned as neither she nor Jake said a word. Jake just didn't want to say anything to make her shut the door on him right away when they got to her room. He could feel the sexual tension in the air between them. He wanted so badly to finally have some private alone time with Amanda where he didn't have to worry about someone seeing them or walking in on them.

Amanda fumbled with her keys trying to get the door to her room open, worried about how exposed they still were standing in the open hallway where anyone could come out of another room or see them from the parking lot below. Finally they were inside putting the laundry bags on the bed. She turned to thank Jake and found herself in his arms. He'd known he had one shot at this and wasn't going to blow it. As Amanda looked up into his eyes, he reached up his hands to cup her face and lowered his mouth to hers. Amanda knew she could've stopped him at any time. She also knew she wanted this.

Jake kissed her slowly and sweetly, trying to ease the nervousness he could feel radiating off of her. Suddenly, it was as if a damn burst and Amanda threw caution to the wind, throwing her arms around his neck and pressing her length against his. Her tongue came out to play next and Jake found himself spellbound. Here was the hidden gem he'd sensed in her before. She was finally just letting herself go and giving an outlet to the sexual tension that had been brewing between them. Jake couldn't get enough. Their tongues dueled and small sounds of approval were coming from both of them. Jake's hands were roaming all over her back and he knew he was finally going to be able to explore her body like he'd been wanting to for what seemed like forever. Amanda was in heaven. Wow could Jake kiss. His lips were at turns playful and fun and then more serious and searching. Amanda loved being pressed up against his strength and the feel of his hands on her back with his arms cradling her made her feel cherished. At five foot seven she didn't often feel small and womanly, but in Jake's arms it was suddenly different. He was over six feet tall and his frame seemed to fit her perfectly. She knew she was finally feeling what it meant to be with a man as a woman, no longer as a girl with a boy.

Jake had no intention of letting things get out of hand with Amanda tonight, knowing instinctively that letting the relationship progress in stages was the only way to go with her. But he was only human and he did want to finally get his hands all over that lush body of hers. So, he scooped her up in his arms and carried her to the twin bed a couple steps away. Amanda was in heaven. She'd never had a guy pick her up before, let alone like she weighed nothing. Jake quickly knocked the laundry bags off the bed and then they were lying next to each other. Jake's heart was pounding in his chest as his hands finally went where they'd been dying to go. He finally got the chance to get his hands on her breasts. It had been everything in him to restrain himself on the couch earlier when she'd been exploring his chest, but now it was his turn. Amanda sighed her approval into his mouth as his hands moved up under her shirt to her bra covered breasts. She could feel him searching for the opening to her bra and broke their kiss to whisper the answer in his ear. Then she stuck her tongue in his ear and felt him jerk as if he'd had a sudden spasm. Which he had. Jake was so hot for her at that moment that he thought he'd explode. He was close to tossing his earlier good intentions out the door.

Amanda relished the sensations coursing through her body at the touch of Jake's hands on her bare skin. Her bra and shirt hit the floor and she decided his shirt was next. She'd been wanting to see all those manly muscles up close and personal. She'd also wanted her breasts touched so badly that she was practically holding her breath, waiting for Jake to really touch them. She wasn't disappointed. Her breasts were very sensitive and she'd finally found a guy who knew what he was doing. Jake took her breasts in his hands and squeezed them lightly, cupping them together and rubbing his thumbs back and forth across her nipples. Jake was watching Amanda's reaction and couldn't believe how responsive she was to his touch. Her eyes were smoldering and their gazes locked on one another. In the back of her mind, Amanda couldn't believe she wasn't looking away in embarrassment. It was almost like an out of body experience. She'd never experienced anything like it. His touch was just so phenomenal that all she cared about right then was having the sensations continue. Jake loved staring into Amanda's eyes, but he'd been dying a slow death wanting to feast on her breasts. Amanda's nipples had been hard before he'd even touched them, but now they were like pencil erasers. He slowly lowered his head to take his first lick. Amanda moaned loudly and could barely contain herself the pleasure was so intense. Unbelievably, the more he licked her nipples, the more distended they seemed to get. He finally took one in his mouth and sucked on it. Amanda went wild in his arms. Her moans got louder and her body started writhing on the bed. It was fantastic. She looked so beautiful with her hair tousled and her back arched up into his embrace. He'd had no intention of things getting so out of control so quickly, but he found that he just couldn't stop himself.

Then Amanda decided it was time to turn the tables. She pushed Jake onto his back, climbed half on top of him and started licking his nipples. She wondered if she could get a similar reaction from giving a man's nipples some attention. She started by licking one while circling the other with her fingernail, mimicking some of the things he'd done to her. He'd never felt anything so erotic. Then she started sucking his nipples, taking turns with each one. Now he was the one writhing on the bed. She was doing things to him that he'd never experienced. He'd never had a woman play with his nipples the way Amanda was. He had no idea it could feel so good. He couldn't help but moan, "Oh, Mandy."

She loved when he said her name like that.

Amanda knew things were getting out of hand, but she was enjoying it so much she just couldn't help herself. She knew she was playing with fire and she could already feel the singe.

Chapter 7

Just as Jake was reaching to push Amanda's sweats down, the phone in Amanda's room started ringing. Amanda quickly said, "Just ignore it." Jake had no problem with that and was more than happy to continue. The ringing stopped and almost immediately began again. There were no answering machines in the rooms, just the old fashioned phones with the shrill rings. Next, Amanda's cell phone started to ring. Amanda groaned and said, "It's my mother," as she rolled away from Jake onto her back to stare at the ceiling. Talk about a buzz kill. The sound of a cat meowing incessantly was the special ring tone she had programmed on her cell phone just for her mom. It had never seemed more appropriate or more annoying than at this very moment. The cell phone just kept meowing. Then it stopped briefly before starting up again. That was her mom's style. Keep calling and calling, because eventually Amanda would just have to answer. Tonight it was as if Amanda's mom had a sixth sense about what had been going on! The meowing just wouldn't quit.

Jake couldn't help but start laughing and begged her, "Make it stop, please! That wailing cat sound is horrible."

Thankfully the noise suddenly stopped on its own and Jake rolled to his side and propped his head in his hand to take an admiring look at Amanda lying next to him. Amanda quickly realized she was still topless and scrambled for the clothes they'd thrown on the ground. She pulled on her T-shirt and then threw Jake's shirt at him. There was no question that their time was up. As Jake walked to the door with Amanda following, he turned to give her one last kiss. Then as he opened the door he said over his shoulder, "I'm sorry I missed getting a look at those thong underwear on you."

"No worries," Amanda replied. "Tonight was laundry night, remember, so I wasn't wearing any," she said as she closed the door. She heard Jake groan loudly as he walked away and she laughed softly to herself as she turned back to answer the phone that had started ringing again.

Saturday morning came around with Amanda suffering the guilt trip inflicted on her by her mother from last night. She hated lying to her mother, but she couldn't exactly tell her what she'd been doing when she called. Especially after what had happened the last time she'd been at the academy. She'd cried on her mother's shoulder a lot about the mistakes she'd made then and had promised them both that she wouldn't repeat them this time around.

As hard as it was going to be, Amanda had to go back to her mantra about no boys. She had to remember why she was here at the academy and what it meant for her career. Messing around with any guy was bad enough, but an instructor? She was just asking for trouble.

So, Amanda basically stayed in bed most of the day, ignoring the world outside her door. At one point someone knocked on her door, but she just put her pillow over her head and willed them to go away. Late in the afternoon Worthless came by and wouldn't give up pounding on her door. "I know you're in there Harry," he was saying through the door. "We didn't see you last night and we haven't seen you all day. We're all going to St. Simon's Island tonight and we want you to come. Be ready to go to dinner in an hour. I won't take no for an answer." One last pounding on the door was followed by, "One hour Harry."

Worthless was a great guy. They'd hit it off from the very beginning when they'd been the first to get their nicknames in physical training class. He was everything you could ask for in a guy, but Amanda had no interest in him as other than a friend. If she'd been interested in having a relationship in the first place, this really would have frustrated her. Worthless wasn't off limits and it would have been easy for them to get involved. They would have had the kind of relationship that happened all the time at the academy. As it was, she still wished she could understand why she felt chemistry with the wrong guy in her situation, but not with the guy who would otherwise be just about perfect for her. In the big scheme of things she had to be thankful there was no spark with Worthless, especially since she was trying to stick to her no boys rule. Amanda wasn't so sure about his feelings for her though. He was such a flirt. She guessed if there was any interest on his part, it was just for a casual fling. That was easy to shoot down. She didn't do casual and she didn't do flings. She just hated that it was so easy to put Worthless in the friend category, but it was impossible to do the same with Jake. Maybe a night out with some classmates was just what she needed. What the hell. Amanda jumped in the shower and was ready to go when Worthless came back around.

Worthless greeted her with a wolf whistle saying, "You clean up nice, Harry!"

"Thanks," was Amanda's reply as she linked arms with him to walk out to the parking lot. She'd decided on a mini skirt, high heeled sandals and a tank top for a night out at the clubs. Nothing like her usual attire, which was more about comfort over style, she nevertheless had some outfits for just such an occasion. She'd also made more of an effort with her hair than she usually bothered with at the academy and she'd added some dark eye make-up for a little drama. Some dark lipstick finished the look and she definitely felt it reflected her new attitude about having fun with no entanglements. She planned on forgetting all about Jake tonight.

That lasted about as long as it took to get to the second club that night. Once Amanda's eyes adjusted to the lighting, she thought for sure she must have already had more than enough to drink and must be seeing things because there in the corner with a group of people sat Jake Marshall. Knowing she'd actually only had one drink at the first club and only had a soda before that with dinner, she figured her eyes weren't deceiving her. What the hell was Jake doing at this bar on the pier? Sure, it was St. Simon's Island and she knew Jake had rented his house out here, but the bars on the pier were usually where the academy students hung out. It wasn't completely unheard of for instructors to party here, but most avoided it like the plague. She'd figured Jake for being in the latter category. Obviously she was wrong about him. To make matters even worse, some girl was clinging to his arm, looking up at him with a big adoring smile on her face. He appeared to be eating up the attention. He'd glanced over briefly when the group she was with first entered the club, but he didn't so much as acknowledge Amanda's presence. Well, if he wanted to play games, she could play games too. She wasn't the stupid, naive girl she used to be.

Amanda's first stop was the bar. She definitely needed another drink. Next, she turned to Worthless and asked him if he'd like to dance. He didn't even hesitate and the two of them went out on the dance floor and really let loose. They were getting pretty risque in their moves, gyrating against one another, but Amanda just went with it. She hoped Jake was getting an eye full. Soon they were breathless and laughing as they left the dance floor and headed back to the bar. Another classmate asked Amanda to dance and pretty soon she was taking turns dancing with most of the guys in the bar. After all, there were hardly any women around so she was definitely in demand as a dance partner.

After a while though, Amanda's head started pounding and the strain of pretending to have fun while watching Jake out of the corner of her eye all night was catching up with her. She decided she needed some air and left the club to walk down to the pier. She started wondering what she was playing at. Obviously Jake hadn't taken their time together seriously so why should she. She also kept wondering how she could have read him so wrong. It brought back all the bad memories of her last time at the academy and she was kicking herself mentally when she felt someone walk up behind her.

"I was hoping you might decide to take a walk down here," Jake's unmistakable voice floated her way. Amanda had known it was him. She didn't know how or why, but she had known he was approaching before he spoke. She turned to look at him and just studied him quietly. All she could think about was how she could have been so wrong about him? The attraction she felt arcing between them even now couldn't be just her imagination, could it? Was it one sided again and she just didn't recognize it? The feelings had been so different with Jake. How could she be this wrong again?

"I came by your room late this morning looking for you," Jake said.

Amanda remained silent.

"I realized I didn't have a phone number for you or anything and thought maybe we could have spent the day together," Jake continued with a puzzled look on his face. He wasn't sure why she was standing there looking at him and not saying a word.

"Well, I guess you made other plans pretty quickly," Amanda finally said to him.

"Actually, I overheard some of your classmates talking about their plans to come club hopping out here, so I took a chance I might run into you," Jake said, leaning one hip against the railing of the pier in that sexy pose of his.

"You expect me to believe that?" Amanda said with a smirk on her face. "I wasn't born yesterday."

"What are you talking about?" Jake said, completely bewildered. "I just said I wanted to see you today and took the chance that I might run into you tonight."

"So you brought another date? Sure, that makes sense." Amanda said, turning away from him to face the ocean again.

"What date? Are you talking about Shelly? She's not my date. I'm here with another male instructor from the academy. Shelly's just a girl I've met before who happened to show up at the bar tonight. Since we know each other, she ended up sitting at our table. That's it," Jake explained, exasperated.

"Hey, what's with you tonight?" Jake asked as he tried to get Amanda to turn back around and look at him.

"Nothing. It doesn't really matter anyway, does it? It's not like we have a relationship going or anything, right?" Amanda answered, slowly turning to look at Jake.

"I'd like to think we started something special, but I guess I could say the same thing to you after watching you dance with all those guys tonight," Jake said, watching Amanda closely.

"Whatever. We shouldn't have gotten involved in the first place," Amanda said as she went to step past Jake and start walking back along the pier toward the clubs.

"Mandy, please stay," Jake whispered as he put his hand out to gently grip her arm.

Amanda froze. Now he was playing dirty. He had to know by now what calling her Mandy did to her.

"I just wanted to tell you that you look incredible tonight. I was jealous of every guy in there. I wanted to be the one dancing with you," Jake said honestly, hoping he could get her to stay.

Amanda felt her resistance slowly slipping away.

"You know that wouldn't be a good idea. As it is, we're taking a lot of chances that someone will say something about us," Amanda said quietly as she turned back to look at him.

Jake didn't care about any of that right now. He could sense her capitulation.

"Come here," Jake murmured as he slowly pulled Amanda into his arms. He kissed her softly and then with increasing voracity. Amanda clung to him and kissed him back, wanting to forget about everything but this.

"Let me drive you home now," Jake whispered in her ear a short while later as she stood in his embrace.

Amanda shook her head, coming back to reality. "No thanks. I'd better go back with the group I came with," Amanda said, turning to go.

Jake once again stopped her with the lightest touch of his hand on her arm. "They're probably still going to stay a few more hours. Just let me take you back."

"No, Jake," Amanda said more adamantly, turning to take his hand off her arm. She was quickly coming to realize how she had once again almost put her better judgment aside for him. "Besides..."

"Harry?" came a voice out of the dark a few feet back.

Surprised, Amanda quickly turned around. There was Worthless with his hands in his pockets and a strange look on his face. Realizing what he must have witnessed, Amanda reluctantly answered, "Yes."

"Everything OK here? I was just coming to check on you, make sure you're all right," Worthless said, wondering what scene he'd just stumbled on.

"Thanks. I'm fine. I'was just about to come back inside actually," Amanda said as she started walking toward Worthless.

Jake remained silent, not wanting to call more attention to himself.

Amanda just threw a quick "Good night" over her shoulder to Jake as she linked arms with Worthless and walked back up the pier toward the clubs.

"Was that who I think it was?" Worthless asked.

"How about you forget you saw anything," Amanda said back, elbowing him in the ribs.

"I can do that, but you'll owe me," Worthless responded cheekily. After a moment he added, "You're asking for trouble. You know that, right?" suddenly sounding a lot more serious.

Amanda just hung her head and didn't reply.

"I hope you know what you're doing Harry," Worthless tried again, showing he was worried for her.

"Actually I don't know that I do, but I'm leaving with you aren't I?" Amanda said, smirking up at him.

"That you are. Lucky me!" Worthless said with a laugh, quickly snapping out of being serious and back into his usual easy going state. He then put his arm around Amanda and led her toward the club their group was now at.

Jake just looked on in frustration. He'd seen her with this guy Worthless a little too much already and now the guy showed up as if she needed rescuing? He wondered what was going on there. Then he had to watch them go from linked arms to Worthless putting his arm around her and hugging her close. Jake could feel his hands turning into fists. He just better hope the guy wasn't the type to blab about what he saw tonight. If word got around about him and Amanda, he knew he would lose his teaching job here at the academy. Then, if he was lucky enough to be able to keep his career intact, he'd get sent to the equivalent of Timbuktu for sure. He'd known that accepting the job at the academy meant he'd be giving up his position in the New York Field Office. It was a risk he'd been willing to take because after his stint as an instructor he was supposed to be able to get first pick of whatever field office had an opening. Being able to transfer to the location of your choice was supposed to be the reward for doing time in Glynco, Georgia. If he left here in shame though, he'd be lucky if they let him occupy a desk at the worst possible field office location--hence Timbuktu. Jake figured he better cut his losses and call it a night...and try to put Amanda out of his mind. Preferably permanently.

Easier said than done.

Monday morning rolled around bright and early. At the start of physical training class, Amanda was nowhere to be seen. Jake asked the class if anyone knew why she was absent and Worthless answered with, "She had to go to the medical clinic this morning." Jake just stared at Worthless for a few seconds. It figured that Worthless would be the one to know the answer, Jake thought, gnashing his teeth. He had to let it go because he had a class to teach. If she didn't show up for defensive tactics training this afternoon, he'd find out what was going on.

Amanda was not looking forward to the impending confrontation with Jake. She knew it was coming, but she was helpless to prevent it. She didn't want to hear the I told you so she was sure to get from Jake when he found out what had happened after she refused to leave with him on Saturday night. If only she had left with him.

So, she tried to make her way into the mat room that afternoon for defensive tactics training without calling attention to herself, but once she saw that both Jake and Donovan were already there she knew it was pointless.

"Over here Harry," Donovan said in his booming voice, waving her over to where he and Jake were standing.

"Why'd you miss this morning's class?" Donovan asked, not lowering his voice or anything. Good thing the rest of the class already knew the story, Amanda thought with a grimace.

"I got hurt over the weekend and had to have it checked out. Here's my note," Amanda held out the small slip of paper she'd been given from the medical clinic. She tried to keep her focus on Donovan and not think about the fact that Jake was just standing there silently watching the exchange.

"This isn't kindergarten Harry. Forget the note. What's the injury? You look fine. You better not be trying to get out of physical training class by making something up," Donovan said while he was looking her up and down.

Amanda could feel the heat of embarrassment creeping up her neck into her face in response to the accusation. However, it also pissed Amanda off enough that she simply lifted her shirt and slightly pulled down her shorts to expose the ugly bruise on her left hip. It was a gigantic black mass that looked absolutely horrible. It spanned almost her whole hip, front to back, and was literally jet black with the start of some yellow, green and blue coloring on the outer edges.

Jake drew his breath in quickly in an audible gasp when he saw the injury and Amanda cringed, still trying to pretend that he wasn't there witnessing her humiliation.

Donovan on the other hand exclaimed, "Damn Harry. That's a hell of a bruise. What the hell happened?"

"Things got a little out of hand at a club on Saturday night. I got caught in the crossfire and had my hip slammed against the bar. The doctor says it's a type of injury that football players get a lot. It should be fine, nothing permanent," Amanda explained as quickly as possible.

"That'll teach you to drink too much," Donovan said loudly.

"I wasn't drunk and it wasn't my fault. I was just in the wrong place at the wrong time," Amanda said with her face getting more red by the minute.

"Whatever Harry. Let's get this class started. You better keep up," Donovan said threateningly.

"Yes sir," Amanda said and almost saluted as she went to find Bulldog, her partner by default. They were working on handcuffing techniques and since they were the only two females in the class they were partnered with one another every time. She carefully kept from looking at Jake throughout the duration of the class. He also didn't come around to her side of the mat room during that afternoon of training. Donovan was a little less hands on too, which was a welcome change. Hopefully he'd finally gotten the message that she wasn't interested and never would be. Of course, as vain as he was she couldn't be sure.

Amanda was just breathing a sigh of relief at the end of class being called when she quickly realized she'd relaxed too soon.

"Harry, see me in my office after your last class of the day," Jake called as she was on her way out the door.

Amanda stiffened for a moment and then answered, "Yes sir," as she continued out the door.

"What do you want to see Harry for," Donovan asked Jake.

"We need to determine how severe her injury is and what she should and shouldn't be doing," Jake answered.

"No way man. You know the drill. Every student has to keep up with the class or risk failing out. If she can't handle it, she shouldn't be here."

"You saw that bruise. Cut her some slack. She still kept up today, didn't she?" Jake replied, getting angrier and angrier with Donovan.

"Just do your job man," Donovan said, shaking his head.

"Don't worry about it. I'll handle it," was Jake's final say as he left the mat room.

Shortly after the end of the day, Jake heard a knock on his office door. His heart started beating faster just knowing that it was probably Amanda.

"Come in," Jake called out.

Amanda walked in to what was more of a closet than an office. The door she'd just opened hit the wall to her left and two small desks, side by side with barely any room between them, were up against the opposite wall. If Amanda sidestepped a few steps, she'd already be up against one of the desks. There were no windows and if the chair of the second desk had been occupied instead of pushed in there would barely have been any room for Amanda to stand.

"Nice digs. You really rate," was the first thing Amanda said to Jake.

Jake remained seated in his cheap government chair and just looked at her for a moment. Amanda tried really hard not to start squirming under his scrutiny. One thing she was good at though was not letting her feelings show if she really tried. So, she summoned up her best cop persona and stood her ground waiting for Jake to say what he was going to say.

"I wanted to talk to you about your injury," Jake finally said.

"What about it?" Amanda said flippantly.

"It looked pretty bad and I just want to make sure you should really be participating in the physically demanding classes," Jake answered, ignoring her attitude.

"It'll be fine," Amanda said with determination.

"Close the door please," Jake asked quietly.

"I'd rather not," Amanda answered back. Jake just gave her a look that spoke volumes and she decided to comply with his request.

Jake stood up to be able to look her in the face and said, "Mandy, this is me you're talking to. I just want to make sure you're not going to be doing irreparable damage here."

Jake noticed a slight change in her eyes when he'd called her Mandy. They'd gone from more of a brown to a slight shade of green. Little did she know how expressive her hazel eyes were. Other than that there was no change in her demeanor.

"I appreciate your concern, but I'll be fine. Is that all?" Amanda said, hoping to put an end to this torture as soon as possible.

"No, that's not all. I care about you, can't you see that?" Jake said in frustration.

Amanda turned away but realized that because the space was so cramped she had nowhere to go.

Jake came up close behind her and said softly, "That bruise is wicked Mandy and I know it's gotta hurt. Just take it easy, OK?"

Amanda took a deep breath and turned to look at Jake. They were so close now that their bodies were almost touching one another.

"No I told you so's?" Amanda asked, not believing that he wasn't going to say more.

"What do you mean?" Jake responded in bewilderment.

"I mean, if I'd left with you that night the way you'd wanted me to, none of this would have happened," Amanda explained.

Jake just shrugged and said, "It's done, so let's not waste time on the what ifs. I just care about what you do about it now." Their faces were so close that Amanda couldn't help but see the sincerity in his expression.

"Thanks Jake," Amanda said, almost feeling like she wanted to cry. She suddenly looked so miserable and just kind of let her shoulders slump. Obviously she'd come to his office expecting something else. Now it was almost as if she was slightly leaning towards him in relief. It could be the cramped space making it seem that way, but Jake went on instinct and just put his arms around her.

It felt so good to be held in his arms. When Jake's arms came around her, Amanda simply put her head on his chest and returned the embrace. She wrapped her arms around him and as soon as Jake felt her response, he tightened his arms and basically gave her a big bear hug. This is what she'd needed yesterday when she'd spent all day in pain wondering what was going to happen if she couldn't get out of bed on Monday morning. It felt so good to just have him holding her. She hadn't realized until that moment how truly alone she'd been feeling.

Jake slowly pulled back and put his hands on her face, cupping her cheeks and lifting her face up to receive his kiss. He kissed her gently and meant to leave it at that, but then Amanda parted her lips and slipped her tongue into his mouth. Once again all his good intentions were gone in an instant. He just couldn't resist the invitation and pulled her in tight to kiss her with all the feelings inside him bubbling over. There was just something about Amanda that got to him like no other woman ever had.

Amanda loved this show of affection from Jake. His kisses were so good, so special. She just didn't know how else to describe them. She'd never felt this way kissing any other guy. She'd been so sure that he was going to berate her, but instead he'd been caring and wonderful. She needed this from

Jake right now. She loved being in his arms and she just couldn't seem to get enough.

Suddenly the door to the office started to open inward and Jake and Amanda jumped apart. Donovan bellowed something down the hall to someone and that gave them the few precious seconds they needed to right themselves. Jake sat back down in his chair to hide his body's obvious reaction to that kiss and Amanda tried everything in her power to keep from turning three shades of red in embarrassment. As soon as Donovan fully opened the door and started to enter, Amanda brushed by him and got out of there and the gym as quickly as possible.

Chapter 8

The week continued on with the usual routine. Jake saw Amanda at least twice a day, for physical training in the morning and defensive tactics in the afternoon. He'd occasionally catch a glimpse of her at the chow hall, but there were no more sightings at the gym. Apparently she was taking it easy to give her hip time to heal. He was glad, but at the same time he couldn't help wondering where they stood after the kiss in his office. He still didn't have her phone number so he couldn't call her and it wasn't wise to approach her with other students around.

On Thursday, he knew he'd finally found the opportunity he needed to get a chance to talk to her.

Amanda was used to having different instructors at the shooting range every time. She knew they must rotate everyone regularly because the instructors were never consistent. During the first round of shooting at the firing line, she sensed the instructors standing back as usual, assessing the shooting abilities of all the students.

Here we go, thought Amanda, as she felt an instructor's presence over her left shoulder. As the shooting progressed, she invariably had one instructor glued to her side trying to give her tips on improving her shot. She'd noticed her last time at the academy as well as now, that the female students were often the one's to get this individual attention. Sure enough, every time at the range it was the same. If only the instructors were consistent in what advice they gave. Last time she'd listened to them all and ended up shooting worse than when she'd started the academy. This time around she'd learned to tune them out. She was already a good shot and knew the instructors didn't really need to be watching over her shoulder the way they always did.

"Nice shooting," came the compliment over her left shoulder as the instructor moved closer to be heard.

Amanda turned her head sharply to the left in surprise and stared straight into Jake's smiling face. She'd know that voice anywhere. He'd caught her completely off guard, since it was the one place she'd never have expected to encounter him.

"What are you doing here?" Amanda asked.

"Filling in for an instructor who's out sick," Jake replied, still smiling. He'd enjoyed her surprise at seeing him!

"Don't tell me you're a certified firearms instructor too?" she said, knowing full well he'd have to be to fill in at the range.

"Yup. I was a firearms instructor with my former agency. I've kept up on the recertifications, so when someone calls in sick I fill in for them on the shifts I have available." He left out the fact that he'd known he would be covering for her class and had jumped at the chance.

"You're just full of surprises, aren't you?" Amanda said.

"You have no idea," Jake said with a slightly wicked grin. Amanda felt herself turning red in embarrassment at the innuendo in that statement and turned away to look down range.

Jake noticed her slightly flushed face and how she'd turned away from him right away. She always had this interesting mix of super confident woman verses shy woman underneath. It continued to intrigue him and he found her blushes oddly endearing.

"So, how've you been?" Jake asked, in an attempt to get her talking again.

Amanda continued to look down range, waiting for the next set of instructions from the lead firearms instructor.

"OK," she replied, not looking at Jake. She hated that telltale blush of hers that she could never control.

"I haven't seen you at the gym this week. I hope that means you've been giving your hip time to heal."

"I have been lying low. Plus we had a few tests this week so I actually had to crack open a book," Amanda joked.

"Yeah, I heard one guy failed out. He couldn't pass one of the law exams, huh?" Jake said.

"You heard right. The first law exam and we've already lost one guy." Amanda said, shaking her head sadly. "They gave him a chance to retest, but he blew it." Everyone was given a chance at one retest after failing anything, sometimes as soon as the next day. Often the pressure was so intense at that point though that they still couldn't manage a passing score in the end.

"I take it the exam wasn't a problem for you?" Jake asked, already knowing the grade she'd gotten. All instructors were kept informed on how students were doing in all aspects of their training at the academy. Naturally, Amanda's name always jumped off the page whenever he got the updates now, so he knew her scores.

"No. Not that it was easy or anything, but I wasn't really worried." Amanda replied.

The lead firearms instructor then started giving instructions for the next round of shooting. Amanda tried to forget about Jake standing right behind her, but talk about adding stress to the situation!

"Nice group," Jake said to Amanda after the round of shooting was over. She had a nice little golf ball sized grouping of bullet holes on her target, right in the center. Damn this woman could shoot, Jake thought to himself. Now that was definitely another added turn on! Not that he needed any more incentives where she was concerned. He fully realized what an amazing woman she was turning out to be. He was beginning to wonder if she even had any weaknesses...knowing full well that everyone did. He better start finding those out, because she was beginning to preoccupy his every thought. Even knowing he was standing over her shoulder hadn't seemed to faze her. She sure was full of surprises herself. She was shooting as well as any of the instructors would if they were on the shooting line. She really was incredible and Jake had an entirely new respect for her and what she brought to the job.

"Thanks," Amanda replied, ducking her head almost as if the compliment embarrassed her. Modest too, thought Jake. She'd had one of the highest grades in the class on the law exam he'd asked her about, but he would never have known that by her answer. She was obviously one of the best shooters in the class too, but he didn't hear her bragging like some of the other guys.

Amanda took off her hearing protection and started loading up her magazine clips with more ammunition for the next round of fire. She was definitely not used to getting compliments from instructors, or any compliments in general really. She was never really sure how to respond. She was very aware of Jake still standing close by, but tried to act like it didn't matter. As she was continuing to load her clips, Jake got even closer and started talking softly into her left ear. It was very loud in the indoor range they were using today, as all the instructors and students voices echoed. She knew it looked like Jake was simply giving her instructions on her shooting. It was nothing out of the ordinary for an instructor to lean in close to make sure he was being heard. In his case, though, he was so close she could feel his breath in her ear. It was sending tingles all down her neck and arms. Normally she hated people crowding into her personal space, which is usually what drove her crazy about the other firearms instructors. It was different with Jake though. She'd definitely never experienced these sensations. He was making her tense up for a whole different set of reasons.

"I'm sorry, what?" Amanda asked when she realized Jake was asking her for an answer to something for the second time. She'd completely missed what he'd been saying!

"I was asking about tomorrow?" Jake said, enjoying her scent this close up. Substituting at the range was working out even better than he'd hoped!

"Uh, sure." Amanda replied, distracted by all the things going on at once. He had her so off guard that she didn't know what she was really responding to.

The lead firearms instructor called out to ready the line of shooters. Amanda hurried to get her hearing protection back in place and her head back in the game. She knew it was going to be everything in her to concentrate and continue to shoot well.

This time at the end of the round of shots fired, Jake came up and pretended to direct her to hold her left arm at a different angle. Goose bumps appeared on her arm and she just stood there frozen at the sensations he was sending through her body with the most basic touch. She wondered if he even knew what he was doing to her.

Jake smiled to himself when he felt the goose bumps on Amanda's arm. Not so cool and calm after all, he thought triumphantly. Then he leaned close to her ear to be heard despite the hearing protection, but making sure no one else could overhear. "I'll pick you up at seven," he said, before going back to standing behind her.

What just happened? was all Amanda could think to herself. Obviously she'd somehow agreed to something tomorrow night at seven.

Friday night rolled around and Amanda was wondering what she was getting ready for. This was supposed to be laundry night! However, she knew she'd inadvertently agreed to something tonight at seven, but she had no idea what. Part of her wanted to refuse to go anywhere and pretend ignorance that she'd even agreed to anything. The other part of her was secretly looking forward to what Jake might have in store. So, she just put on a nice pair of blue jeans with a black formfitting top. Not too casual and not too dressy. Hopefully appropriate for whatever Jake had planned. She'd blown her hair out into softer, bigger curls, instead of her usual wash and go wavy look during class times. She had on a light amount of make up to finish off the casual look she was going for.

Once she was ready, Amanda started becoming increasingly nervous about someone seeing her with Jake tonight. Hopefully he was thinking of that too and was taking her somewhere no one else would think to go. She knew they'd risked being seen together before, but that had always been unplanned. This time was different. It was a planned date. She started wondering what the hell she was thinking, taking the risk. She knew she was considered a probationary employee and could be fired for the littlest impropriety. Being caught dating an instructor was no little impropriety either. Oh well. There was no use dwelling on it now. So, she decided to head downstairs and at least keep Jake from coming up to her room.

Thankfully Friday night meant the academy was usually a ghost town. This was when Amanda wished she had her own car the most. After being cooped up in such a high stress environment during the week, as soon as the weekend rolled around everyone just wanted to make a break for it. Most people headed right to the pier on St. Simon's Island to start partying. Just far enough to feel like you were getting away from it all.

Jake pulled up in a black jeep, just as Amanda came down the stairs. She quickly jumped in as if it was some sort of stealth mission they were on. Thankfully he had the air conditioning on so she was no longer in danger of completely melting. It was another hot, humid night in Georgia.

"Hi. You look beautiful," was Jake's greeting as he once again admired the natural beauty that shone from Amanda.

Amanda blushed and responded with a "Thank you."

Her nerves were still trying to get the best of her so she quickly asked, "Where are we going?"

"You'll see. Just sit back and relax. Enjoy the drive," Jake responded, seeming completely relaxed behind the wheel.

It was a nice drive, which she began to appreciate once she realized they were going in a direction she'd never been before. Beautiful, old weeping willow trees were on either side of the slightly winding road. She could see the marsh area through the trees and soon it seemed like the wetlands were on both sides of the road and they had left civilization behind. Not a house was in sight, just the swamp.

After a while, they pulled up to a restaurant that seemed to be an extension of the landscape. It was built on stilts and jutted out over the marsh into the bayou. Amanda was immediately enchanted and felt like if she had blinked, she would have missed it altogether.

Amanda turned to Jake and asked, "How do you even know about this place?"

Jake smiled and answered, "It's a local secret. They have great food and as you can see the ambiance is unique. Hope you're hungry!"

Jake jumped out of the jeep and came around to open the car door for Amanda.

"Thank you," Amanda said, putting her hand into Jake's outstretched one.

"You're welcome. You jumped in so quickly when I came to pick you up that I didn't get a chance to get the door for you then," Jake teased with a smile.

"Well, you're quite the gentleman. Your mom must be proud," Amanda said, secretly impressed by this chivalrous behavior that she'd never been treated to before by any of the other guys she'd dated.

"She is. She definitely raised me to have good manners," Jake replied as he kept hold of her hand and started up the dark brown wooden ramp to the restaurants front door.

Jake held open the front door for Amanda and she preceded him into the restaurant and felt like she was entering a pirate's lair of old. It was very dark, with wall sconces giving off a muted yellow glow. There was pirate paraphernalia on the walls, tastefully done to encourage the other worldly feeling the setting was obviously going for.

Jake mentioned the reservation he'd made at the reception desk in the front entry way and they were immediately taken down a dimly lit hallway to one of the tables on the screened in porch, overlooking the bayou.

"This place is amazing," Amanda said to Jake while gazing out at the water. There was almost a full moon, its light reflecting off the water. This combined with the outside lights of the restaurant to provide an almost eerie ambiance. With the crickets and frogs in the background, making the steady sound she'd always associated with the swamp, it felt like she'd been transported back in time.

Jake just watched Amanda as she was taking in the scenery. He felt like the luckiest guy to be sitting there with her, finally on their first official date.

"I thought you'd like it here. It is pretty unique and not many people know it exists," Jake said once her focus was back on him.

"I love the pirate angle! I know Georgia's got quite a bit of pirate history." Amanda said, completely enchanted by the surroundings.

"Yes, and who doesn't love a good pirate story!" Jake said with the slightly wicked grin she'd seen once before.

Amanda could feel herself start to blush at the innuendo. Good thing the lights were down low.

After ordering some of the local specialty dishes, one with crawfish and one with shrimp, Amanda and Jake finally spent some time really getting to know each other.

"So, you know Mark Mitchell, our firearms instructor at the Los Angeles Field Office?" Amanda asked as the conversation turned to their current jobs.

"Yeah. We actually went through criminal investigator training together years ago. The same one you're in now. We sat next to each other and really became good friends. I actually consider him to be one of my best friends now."

"Of course!" Amanda exclaimed as it dawned on her. "Marshall and Mitchell...you guys definitely would have been seated next to each other!" Amanda chuckled softly.

"Yeah. Things haven't changed much, have they! Still the same set up for each class. Everyone seated in alphabetical order," Jake said, laughing with her.

"I'm seated next to David Grygierczyk. You know him as "Alphabet" thanks to your fellow instructor Donovan. Not that it isn't an appropriate nickname! David's last name is quite a mouth full!" Amanda said, chuckling some more.

Jake loved the sound of her laughter and once again found himself wanting to hear more of it.

"Then, on my right I've got Lewis Jackson, who has managed up until now not to be gifted with a nickname. He rarely says anything though, so I guess it's not surprising that he's managed to stay under the radar," Amanda continued, describing the every day classroom set up.

Jake knew what a drag it was to always be in the same classroom with the same people on either side of you day after day. The classes he taught were actually the only one's where you got some choice in who you had next to you and whether you wanted to be in the front row or not. So it was easy for him to commiserate.

Amanda realized at this point what a good time she was having with Jake. She was really enjoying the conversation and realized they were finding out a lot about each other. He was a good listener and seemed genuinely interested in what she had to say. He also shared things about himself and so far it didn't seem like any topic was taboo. They'd talked about their families, schools, why'd they'd made the choices that had led them to their current careers. They had basically filled in a lot of the blanks, considering their new relationship. They'd even touched on the future a bit and found out that they had similar goals and dreams. The conversation flowed easily and there was never a dull moment or an awkward silence.

"You know, I just have to tell you how impressed I was with your shooting the other day. You're better than some of the firearms instructors I know," Jake said to Amanda.

"I'll mention that to Mark when I get back," Amanda said with a twinkle in her eye.

"Very funny. I'm sure he's already seen you in action and been impressed himself," Jake replied.

"He did take me out to the range before I left for the academy to make sure I knew what I was in for as far as qualifying. He wanted to run through the course of fire requirements and let me know what score I'd need to pass and all that. He was great and I totally appreciated him doing that. It eased my mind about the firearms portion of the academy."

"Yeah, he's really good about helping people out in any way he can. I'm surprised you two haven't gotten better acquainted?" Jake said casually.

"What's that supposed to mean?" Amanda asked, knowing full well what he was fishing for.

"He's a single guy, you haven't mentioned a recent ex-boyfriend, and I know he would have at least hit on you!"

Amanda started laughing. "You do know him well. He's quite the player," Amanda said evasively, trying to think fast on how she could get out of this line of questioning.

"I believe he was still involved in a relationship at the time, wasn't he?" She said, attempting to distract him from his original question.

"You're right," Jake said, considering the time frame in which they would have met. "Except it's more like he was trying to extricate himself from a quasi relationship at the time! I think after this last crazy one, his player days are going to be over."

"Oh really? Seems like you guys must chat quite a bit if you know all that." Amanda couldn't help but ask.

"Yeah, we try and catch up with each other regularly. Like I said, we've become best friends over the years."

Amanda excused herself at this point to use the restroom and no sooner had she left the table than the doubts started moving in. She started lecturing herself on how stupid she was being to get involved like this again, as if she still hadn't learned the lessons of the past. Even if he was a great guy, there was no future in it. She was going back to California after the 12 weeks were up and he was an instructor at an academy that was 3000 miles away. Not to mention his connection to Mark. Mark was the firearms instructor at her field office. Why was she just now realizing that Mark and Jake may have discussed her already or probably would at some point? She knew what a small community law enforcement was. There was the potential once again for everyone to easily find out her personal business. Why was she going down the same road toward repeating the same mistakes? This was a worse disaster than she'd even realized.

Amanda was shocked to see the time on the clock in the hallway as she was returning to the table. She couldn't believe how much time had elapsed since Jake had picked her up at the academy.

"Do you know what time it is?" Amanda asked when she got back to the table.

"Time flies when you're having fun?" Jake quipped. "You don't turn into something else at the stroke of midnight do you?"

"Ha. Ha." Amanda replied. "I just want to try and avoid the line up of cars at the security gates, waiting to get back into the academy."

"Sure, that's probably wise." Jake replied. He could sense something was different since she'd come back from the restroom, but he couldn't figure out what might have changed in the few minutes she had been gone.

"Thank you for dinner. It was delicious and I loved the restaurant." Amanda said on the drive back.

"You're very welcome. I'm glad you enjoyed it." Jake replied. They continued with some small talk but were mostly silent after that.

Jake had tried to steal a few more minutes with her outside the restaurant. He'd been wanting so badly to kiss her again and had been waiting for the right time. Amanda had been too worried about getting back though and had rushed him to the car.

As they came up to the security gates at the entrance to the academy Jake said, "I guess you were right to be worried. What's with all the cars?"

Amanda had been afraid this might happen. Sometimes visitors came on the weekends and hadn't yet gotten the proper passes for their vehicles or their visitor identification badges. So, the security guards had to search the vehicles and administer the proper passes before they could be allowed to enter through the academy gates. This caused a back up of cars along the road leading to the security checkpoint. Also, there was invariably going to be someone who forgot their identification badge, which everyone in the vehicle had to have to show the guards before being allowed to enter. That meant another delay.

At least on the weekends they had both sides of the security check point open. Of course, that also meant that you were lined up with other cars waiting to enter the academy. They were also hitting one of the busy times where people were coming back with the alcohol to finish getting drunk close to their rooms instead of out at the bars. This all increased the possibility that someone would recognize them and make note of the fact that they were together.

There were enough cars that Amanda was really getting the jitters. The last thing she needed now was to get in trouble for being with Jake when she'd decided that it wasn't going to happen again.

"Guess I haven't had much reason to be coming back to the academy at this hour so I've forgotten what it's like," Jake said as he turned to look at Amanda.

"I just don't want anyone making an issue of us being seen together," Amanda said worriedly.

"Just relax. Most of these people are too drunk to remember anything by morning!" Jake jokingly said, knowing that Amanda was right to be concerned. Being lined up waiting for entrance to the academy along with a bunch of cars filled to the max with students was not ideal.

They finally made it through the gate with no incident they were aware of. Jake was just pulling into the parking lot in front of Amanda's barracks when she said, "You don't need to park or bother getting out. I think it's best if I just jump out and we call it a night."

"Let me at least walk you back to your room. After all, that's what a proper gentleman would do," Jake said, the kiss he had so been looking forward to still on his mind.

"I appreciate you being chivalrous Jake, I really do. In this instance though, I think self-preservation takes precedence. We don't need to take any more chances on being seen together than we've already taken tonight."

Jake decided not to push and agreed not to get out of the car, but he parked and said, "Can I at least get your phone number so I can call you?"

"Sure," Amanda said, taking the path of least resistance, and waited while he programmed it into his cell phone. She considered giving him a wrong number, but since she'd be seeing him again every weekday for class, she didn't think that would be a wise move.

"Thanks again for dinner," Amanda said as she went to open the car door.

"Mandy," Jake said, reaching out to her. As she turned her head to look back at him, Jake used his right hand to cup her chin and pull her into the kiss he was already half way leaned in for.

Amanda couldn't resist his plea and leaned toward him until their lips met. He kissed her softly and sweetly and she started feeling like she wanted to cry. Then she figured if this was going to be it for them, she might as well make it good. So, she grabbed his shirtfront with both hands and really poured herself into the kiss. All of a sudden her tongue was invading his mouth and Jake went from barely caressing a kitten to holding onto a tigress. She sure was full of surprises, he thought yet again, but he definitely wasn't going to object. So, Jake fisted his hands in her hair and kissed her back with all the emotions he was feeling as well.

Too soon Amanda was pulling back and saying she had to go.

Jake smiled at her with that slightly wicked grin of his and said, "Are you sure I can't walk you up to your room?"

Amanda just had to laugh. He was so darn cute and that kiss had been a-m-a-z-i-n-g!

"I'm sure," Amanda said as she now quickly got out of the car.

Jake watched her run to the stairs that would take her to the upper floor of the barracks and kept watch until he saw her open the door to her room and go in safely. She sure kept him on his toes and he didn't know what to make of how their night had ended. Now he had her phone number though and he couldn't wait to talk to her about it tomorrow. He drove home with a big grin on his face. Who wouldn't after a kiss like that!

Chapter 9

Saturday mornings were her favorite because she finally got to sleep in until whenever she wanted. There was always a lot of noise in the barracks when most people started getting up. Doors slamming combined with loud conversations in the open hallway outside her room were par for the course. Thankfully, she was usually able to just roll over, put a pillow over her head and go back to sleep.

Not so, this particular morning. Once the door slamming started, Amanda found herself wide awake lying on her back and staring at the ceiling. Physically she was exhausted, but mentally she was off and running. She was trying not to think about last night, but couldn't help replaying the conversation they'd had at dinner. They had so much in common. Then there was that amazing kiss at the end of the night. She knew she'd never had that kind of chemistry with anyone else. She couldn't seem to stop herself from obsessing about Jake and what last night had meant.

By 10 a.m. she'd already looked at her phone twice to see if he'd called yet--as if she might have missed it.

What was the matter with her? This was completely opposite to what she'd decided on at the end of last night. At one point she hadn't even wanted to give him her phone number. Now she was waiting for him to call? She was so completely irritated with herself at this point. Her head and heart seemed to be fighting a losing battle.

Finally she just got out of bed, put on some running clothes and decided to go for a jog. She knew that the only way to build up stamina for all the running during physical training classes was to just get out and do it. She hated it, but the more she did it the better she performed when it was time for another road march. She was also partially torturing herself in the hopes that she'd stop thinking so much about Jake. Leaving her cell phone behind was a good start. At least she wouldn't be glancing at it every five minutes.

By the time she got back to her room she was soaked in sweat and a little more clearheaded about how she wanted her weekend to play out. When she saw that he still hadn't called she stomped to the bathroom door to take a shower. Of course, Bulldog was in the bathroom, which meant she'd have to wait. Now she was getting just plain cranky. All she wanted was a nice cool shower. Of course Bulldog would pick this Saturday to still be hanging out in her room and using the bathroom. Usually she was long gone by now. Then, in the middle of this new aggravation of the day, the phone rang. It was finally Jake calling.

"Hope I'm not calling too early," Jake asked, trying not to laugh since it was almost noon. "I remember you telling me last night about how much you love to sleep in on the weekends."

Amanda remained silent, too cranky at the moment to care about how thoughtful it actually was of Jake to wait to call her because he'd figured she'd been sleeping in.

"I didn't wake you, did I?" Jake asked when he didn't get a response.

"No." Amanda answered curtly.

"OK. Well, I was hoping we could go to dinner again tonight? Maybe we could even get together a little earlier so we don't have to worry about hitting the same traffic jam at the security gates?" Jake asked, willing to overlook her curtness. He remembered how she'd told him last night that she wasn't a morning person. He figured it was probably still morning to her.

Amanda's head had won out over her heart while she had been jogging and she quickly came up with, "Sorry Jake, I already made plans with some of my classmates tonight."

"Oh. OK." Jake said, sounding both sur-prised and disappointed.

Guess he'd thought she was a sure thing. Not again. She wasn't going to be anybody's sure thing ever again.

"Where are you guys going?" Jake asked.

"Probably just the usual places," Amanda answered vaguely.

"Well, since that means St. Simon's Island, I'll probably see you at one of the clubs," Jake said confidently, knowing he could do the same thing he'd done the last time they'd run into each other. St. Simon's Island had their night clubs all lined up, going down the length of the pier. He knew students usually hopped from one club to another and if he stayed put in one club, he was bound to run into her sooner or later. The plan had worked last time!

"Uh, sure. Maybe," Amanda answered, thinking that was the last thing she wanted to have happen. How was she going to avoid that?

"What about Sunday? Maybe we could spend some time together on Sunday?" Jake asked, not giving up easily.

"Maybe. Can we talk about it tomorrow though? I was just waiting for the shower and it's finally available." Amanda said when she heard Bulldog unlocking the bathroom door.

"Sure, I'll call you tomorrow. Around this time tomorrow OK with you?" Jake asked.

Of course he was going to be cool about it. Amanda started to feel even crankier because she knew she wasn't really being fair to him. She should just break things off with him right now. She had her guard back up though and she was going to just play this thing out the way she knew she needed to.

"Yes," Amanda responded and then grudgingly admitted, "I appreciate you remembering what I said last night about liking to sleep in."

"No problem. I'll talk to you tomorrow. Enjoy your day Mandy."

Amanda felt a sharp pain to the heart. That nickname got her every time.

"Thanks Jake. You too. Bye."

Agreeing to go to a bar in Brunswick, the nearest town to the academy, was not one of her better decisions. This became apparent pretty quickly. Not only was the place full of a bunch of locals, but most of them were already completely drunk and getting rowdier by the minute. She'd known when Worthless had mentioned the group plans for tonight that she should probably sit this one out, but after the excuses she'd made to Jake she didn't want to be caught in a lie. Plus, the last thing she needed was a Saturday night locked up alone in her room with tons of time to think. Brunswick also happened to be the perfect solution to worrying about running into Jake on St. Simon's Island. She'd never see him in Brunswick. No one from the academy went to Brunswick if they could help it. She'd never really known why, but she was about to find out.

"Check it out boys, the feds have come slumming."

"What's the matter, you get lost?"

"Hey honey, you come looking for a real man?"

And it went on and on. Most of the rude comments were coming from the bar area so Amanda and their group went to stand at the railing overlooking the dance floor below. This particular club was in an old warehouse with a pretty cool set up. You entered on the top floor where there was a big, long bar. That's where most people were crowded at the moment. Then there was a half moon shaped railing that allowed people to watch those dancing on the first floor below. Stairs on either side of the half moon railing provided access between the two floors.

"You sure are getting a lot of attention Harry," Worthless said to Amanda, nodding to indicate two men in particular who hadn't stopped staring. They were both similar in stature, big and burly. Definitely the bruiser type.

"You'd think they'd never seen a woman before," Amanda replied.

"Probably never one as pretty as you," Alphabet joked. "I'll brave the bar and get us some drinks."

Amanda was grateful for the stand up group of guys she was with. There was always the light hearted girl boy banter going on between them all, but it was always good natured and everyone had realized by now that they were better off being just friends. After the night Worthless had caught Amanda at the pier with Jake, she'd noticed a slight change in him. He still flirted outrageously, but there was no longer a question mark mixed in. It was like he understood she had something else going on and he was content now to just be great friends.

"Do you want to dance?" Worthless asked Amanda. "Might get us away from those two rednecks for a bit." Worthless said, referring to the same two guys who still hadn't stopped staring.

"Why not," Amanda answered and they headed down the stairs to the dance floor.

The music was booming and they'd barely made a spot for themselves on the crowded dance floor when Amanda leaned towards Worthless and yelled in his ear, "Heads up. Tweedledee and Tweedledum just followed us onto the dance floor."

"Roger that," Worthless yelled back.

Sure enough, the two men who'd been staring at her since she'd arrived at the bar tried to cut in and dance with her.

"She's with me," Worthless said to the two bruisers. He was starting to get a bad feeling about this.

"I'm with my boyfriend, guys, but thanks anyway," Amanda was yelling at the two guys, trying to be heard above the music without getting too close.

"One dance isn't too much to ask, is it? Or are you just too good for us?" Tweedledee said, leaning into Amanda and giving her a whiff of his foul breath. Then he grabbed her by the shoulders and tried to pull her in close.

Meanwhile, Tweedledum was trying to put some distance between Worthless and Amanda by running interference for his buddy. Obviously their game plan had changed.

"Listen, I don't want any trouble. We're just here to have a few drinks and a dance or two," Worthless said, trying to reason with Tweedledum.

"One dance with the girl isn't going to cause any trouble. Just back off and you'll get her back when we're finished."

"No can do. Like I said, she's with me," Worthless replied. He signaled the rest of their group still standing at the railing to come down to the dance floor. He had a feeling this was going to get ugly.

At this point, Amanda was also pretty worried about what it was going to take for Tweedledee to take no for an answer. She was pushing on his chest, trying to keep him from pulling her any closer, but he was so inebriated that this tug of war they were engaged in resulted in him losing his balance and falling towards her. She had to use all her strength just to keep them both from toppling over. Now she was clutched in his arms, in the most uncomfortable embrace, as a result.

"I'm just going to go and get a drink right now," Amanda said into the ear right next to her mouth, in a last ditch effort to get herself out of the situation.

"No way honey," was the reply she got.

"Let go now," Amanda yelled into Tweedledee's ear, done trying to be reasonable and not cause a scene.

His arms just tightened around her.

Amanda waited briefly for just the right opening and then kneed him in the groin. He went down, but took her with him! She hadn't counted on that.

Worthless saw this happen and knew Amanda needed help immediately, so he threw a punch at Tweedledum. His fist connected with Tweedledum's face, but he didn't even appear fazed by it and immediately took a swing at Worthless in return. Worthless was so distracted by what was happening to Amanda that he didn't dodge the fist coming at him fast enough. He was hit by a glancing blow to the chin, but it was enough for him to taste blood in his mouth.

The other guys in their group soon came to the rescue. Alphabet and Bill Longovich, nicknamed Shorty, helped get Tweedledum off of Worthless, as the two had graduated to wrestling around on the dance floor. Amanda seemed to have her situation under control. Tweedledee's nose was bleeding and he was lying on the floor with her standing over him. The crowd had parted just enough to be able to watch the action, but it was just a matter of time before all hell broke loose.

As soon as their group was in the clear, Amanda pointed and yelled, "Exit." They all quickly headed out the emergency exit doors on one side of the dance floor. This brought them out into the alley on the opposite side of the club entrance and they all took off in a dead run to get to the car they'd come to the club in.

"Never a dull moment," Worthless said with a bloody grin as he and Amanda jumped into the back seat.

"Unbelievable," Amanda said, shaking her head as Alphabet quickly drove the car out of downtown Brunswick.

"Guess that's why we were lectured at the beginning of the academy about staying away from the local hang outs," Shorty joked from the front passenger seat.

"Yeah, and you ignored the warning and wanted to go anyway," grumbled Amanda, knowing full well she was as guilty as the rest of them.

"Your lip is bleeding," Worthless said to Amanda.

"So is yours," Amanda said back. Then they both started laughing ruefully.

"How'd you get away from that Neanderthal anyway?" Worthless asked Amanda.

"After I kneed him in the groin he took me down with him, but then I head butted him in the nose and that was the end of that," she answered with satisfaction.

"Ouch," said Worthless.

"He picked the wrong woman to mess with, didn't he Harry?" Alphabet said with a laugh.

"Damn right he did," Amanda answered. "Let's just hope since we got out of there without damaging anything at the bar, this incident doesn't come back to haunt us at the academy."

That statement kept everyone quiet for a minute.

"How are we going to explain your appearances if asked?" Shorty wanted to know. "Harry's got a cut lip and Worthless looks like he's been in a bar fight."

"We'll just lie low tomorrow and by Monday you'll hardly be able to tell. My lips cut on the inside and if there's bruising on my chin I'll come up with something. Tweedledum got in some good punches to my chest, but I'll obviously be wearing a shirt so no one will be the wiser," Worthless said to everybody.

"You'll just have to take it easy on me during defensive tactics!" Worthless said, pointing to Shorty.

"No problem, partner. I'll pretend you're a girl," Shorty replied.

"Hey, watch it Shorty. I'm fresh from a fight and I've still got some left in me," Amanda said, reaching forward to push Shorty's shoulder.

"Yeah, you probably do. After all, Alphabet and I had to help out Worthless here. You'd already handled your situation on your own," Shorty said, laughing hysterically with Alphabet joining in.

Worthless just sat there with a sheepish grin on his face. "A few more rounds and I would have had him."

"Keep telling yourself that. I'll take Amanda in my corner any day!" Alphabet chimed in.

"I'll second that," Shorty said in agreement.

"How'd you end up with that cut lip anyway?" Worthless asked Amanda.

"After my groin kick took us down to the ground, the Neanderthal backhanded me and his ring caught my lip. Then he decided he wanted to wrestle some more and that's what he got the head butt to the nose for," Amanda said while rubbing her forehead. She could already feel the headache coming on now that the adrenaline rush was over.

"Let's do this again real soon," Shorty said as they were all getting out of the car in the parking lot in front of their barracks.

"Not," Amanda and Worthless replied simultaneously. Then they all laughed together and Worthless put his arm around Amanda's shoulder asking, "Can you help this old man up the stairs to his room?"

Amanda chuckled and the two of them made their way up to the second floor.

"Thanks for trying to rescue me," Amanda said to Worthless as they were parting at her door.

"Anytime," Worthless said with a wink and an attempt at a smile, his lip already puffed up and his chin showing signs of discoloration. He slowly started down the hallway to his room at the other end, the fight having obviously taken a toll.

Amanda opened her door and watched him for a moment longer to make sure he'd be all right. Then she was closing her door and thinking how she couldn't remember a time when she'd ever been happier to see her eight by eight foot cell, dropping on the bed and immediately falling asleep exhausted.

Chapter 10

Amanda and Worthless followed the plan for Sunday, lying low and pretty much staying out of sight. Alphabet and Shorty snuck food from the chow hall for them so they didn't have to go anywhere. Worthless was pretty beat up and Amanda wasn't looking good either. Most of Worthless' injuries would be hidden by his shirt, but his chin was definitely bruised and his lower lip was twice its normal size. Amanda's wasn't looking too much better. You could definitely tell she had a cut lip. The two of them spent some time Sunday afternoon commiserating over the phone on their various injuries and generally getting to know each other better. They also came up with a plan for Monday morning.

Jake had called as well, but Amanda decided not to answer. She felt terrible about ignoring his calls, but didn't want to have to explain things yet. She hated lying, so if she didn't talk to him she wouldn't have to lie about anything. She was actually hoping she wouldn't have to explain anything at all in the end. If her lip healed a little more over night, no one would be the wiser. She might look fine by tomorrow morning.

Wishful thinking on her part.

Worthless knocked on Amanda's door bright and early Monday morning. He was already in his gym uniform, Alphabet having gone to the gym yesterday to get it for him. It was the first phase of the plan they'd come up with. No time in the gym's locker room for any questions. Phase two was for Worthless to come directly to Amanda's room in the morning. It was unusual for Worthless to skip breakfast, but he had decided to forgo the questions he was sure to get at the chow hall given his appearance. He figured the fewer people that saw him, and the less he interacted with anyone today, the better. Both he and Amanda knew they'd better keep a low profile.

Amanda was already up, her nerves having gotten the best of her this morning. She hadn't hit the snooze button once.

Phase three of their plan was to try and put some make-up over both their injuries before heading directly to the gym. Not very original, but they thought they'd better give it a shot. In the end,

Amanda felt like she should have sent Alphabet or Shorty to the store yesterday to get some better concealer. She rarely wore any make-up and quickly realized what she had on hand definitely wasn't doing the trick. After examining themselves in the mirror they both starting sweating the possible ramifications of having to explain what had happened.

Knowing there was nothing else they could do, they headed off to the gym. Unfortunately, they were both still experiencing the pain from the encounter at the club Saturday night, so they propped each other up with their arms on each others shoulders, using each other like a crutch to hobble along. They made quite the picture together, but it made things a little easier. They'd developed an easygoing friendship that was a lot of fun. Even this morning was no exception. Worthless had her laughing most of the way! It did, however, seem like an extra long walk to the gym for both of them that morning.

They had been debating how the day was going to go. They didn't have long to wait for the answer. The first thing they saw when they entered the mat room for physical training class was Jake Marshall frowning at them both.

"Great," Amanda mumbled under her breath to Worthless as they walked past Jake.

"Fantastic," Worthless mumbled back.

"What's his deal?" Worthless asked Amanda after they'd taken off their shoes and were headed to the back of the room to start stretching.

Amanda just shrugged and added, "He sure seemed happy to see us, didn't he?" knowing part of the reason Jake had been frowning at the two of them as they'd entered the mat room. As much as they may have hoped otherwise, they both still looked banged up from Saturday night. Amanda's bottom lip had a noticeable cut and was still slightly puffy. Worthless had an ugly bruise on his chin and his bottom lip was still swollen. They thought maybe the make-up had hidden some of the evidence. Based on Jake's reaction, they shouldn't even have bothered.

"You two still got something going on?" Worthless asked, as they were sitting across from each other on the mat room floor.

"Shush. No," Amanda said, looking around guiltily, hoping no one had heard what Worthless asked.

"You better tell him that," Worthless commented while halfheartedly stretching, his ribs still hurting pretty bad from the bar fight.

"Shut up, Worthless," Amanda said, knowing she was turning red in embarrassment and trying to signal him to knock it off with a slicing hand motion across her throat.

"I'm just saying..." Worthless continued, getting a kick out of watching Amanda turn different shades of red.

Amanda finally growled in frustration and turned her back on him to continue stretching out in silence. She heard Worthless laughing behind her and tried to ignore him.

She'd already known this morning was going to be uncomfortable, since she'd never returned any of Jake's calls yesterday. Judging by the once over Jake had given her and Worthless though, she might have to raise her estimation of the level of discomfort this day would bring.

"Everybody line up and let's get started," Donovan yelled as he came into the mat room.

"Drop and start with push ups," Jake interjected before Donovan could continue.

Amanda heard Worthless say, "Uh oh" before they all started yelling out the numbers of the push-ups they were counting. It didn't take long for Worthless to start looking very pale. Amanda didn't know how much of a punishment he could survive today. Lucky for him he was in great shape and normally had no trouble keeping up. If he slacked off a little today it hopefully wouldn't stand out too much. She wasn't feeling so great herself either. She knew she needed to participate just enough to stay under the radar.

Sure enough, Jake was in rare form and the class was pushed to the limit, with Jake doing all the exercises right along with them. It always impressed Amanda when the instructors proved that they could not only dole out the punishment, but take it themselves as well. Donovan was of course staying true to form, just yelling from the sidelines but not participating in the exercises. So, as much as she might have wanted to ignore Jake, she found herself admiring him and his style once again. However, by the end of physical training class that day, she was cursing him silently along with everyone else as she dragged herself to the shower stall in the locker room. She had no doubt that they'd all just been punished heavily and she knew she was to blame.

By that afternoon, Jake had heard plenty of scuttlebutt about Harry and Worthless and what had supposedly happened over the weekend. Speculation always ran rampant, especially when there was physical evidence that something had definitely occurred. One only had to look at the two of them to see that there was something to the gossip for sure this time. Bruised faces and cut lips were pretty hard to ignore and in a setting like the academy it became fun gossip to spice up the day.

Lucky for them he hadn't heard about anyone taking the evidence too seriously. They were both exceptional students, so that didn't hurt either.

Amanda had been dreading defensive tactics class most of the day, knowing that she should probably apologize to Jake for not calling him back over the weekend. She definitely felt like she should do something to diffuse the situation, rather than risk facing the punishment of one more of that morning's brand of brutal physical training classes. So, at the end of defensive tactics class she made a point of taking an extra long time putting her shoes on. Donovan had already left the mat room, expecting Jake to lock up as usual and most of the other students were already gone.

Jake quickly realized that Amanda was deliberately taking her time and by the furtive glances in his direction he realized she was waiting to get a chance to talk to him.

Finally it was just the two of them left in the mat room and Jake went to close one door and Amanda the other. Amanda dreaded having to face Jake, but knew she owed him at least that.

"Sorry about not calling you back yesterday." Amanda started off saying.

"What happened to your lip?" Jake asked, not responding to her apology at all.

"Nothing really. It's no big deal." Amanda replied, not making eye contact with Jake.

Jake just stood there staring at her silently. He figured if she couldn't even tell him how she'd gotten hurt, then what was the point of any of this. Was he just wasting his time?

Amanda was getting more embarrassed by the minute, especially when Jake remained silent. She glanced at him guiltily and saw that he was just staring at her with a look she couldn't quite define.

"Something stupid happened on Saturday night. Like I already said, it was no big deal." Amanda said in a rush, just trying to get it all over with. Technically the less she told him the better. He was, after all, an instructor at the academy.

"Something happened to both you and Worthless? And if it was no big deal, then why avoid my calls on Sunday?" Jake fired back.

Amanda just shrugged her shoulders and said nothing more.

Jake tried one more time to get something more from her by saying, "It seems like every time we get close you end up doing something stupid to try and put some distance between us. Why?"

Amanda suddenly felt like he'd just slapped her. At the same time she realized he was only using her own words against her. She couldn't blame him.

"You're right. I do." Amanda hung her head as she said it and then geared up for what she knew she had to do.

"I'm sorry. This just isn't going to work. We shouldn't have gotten involved in the first place and we both know it. So, let's just try to move forward as instructor and student again and leave the rest behind." Amanda was proud of herself for stating it clearly and looking Jake in the face as she did.

Jake couldn't believe what had just come out of her mouth. He should have been forewarned though. Her face had suddenly become expressionless and her eyes had gotten a far away look, as if she'd removed herself emotionally from the conversation.

"No problem, Harry," Jake replied and started heading toward the door.

Amanda felt poleaxed by his use of that horrid nickname.

Jake held the door open and turned off the lights as soon as she passed him. She stood there watching him lock up and wasn't sure what else to say. She need not have worried, since he just turned his back on her and walked off down the long hallway. As she watched him go, she knew in her head that she'd made the right decision. Her heart was a different matter. All the while she'd felt as though her heart was breaking.

Chapter 11

The next few weeks were some of the most difficult for Amanda. She felt tired all the time, not only physically but mentally as well. Initially, after what had happened with Jake, she tried not to think about it all too much. She made a valiant effort to put it all behind her. The problem was that she saw him for classes at least twice a day. There he was, larger than life, right in her face.

They both seemed to ignore each other at first, but then there were times when they'd catch one another stealing a longer than normal look. She hadn't wanted to examine her feelings for him too closely, but in the end she realized she was sad every time she thought about what could have been. Then she became increasingly depressed about it. No surprise, since she'd also had a lot of extra time to think lately. She was spending a lot more time in her room alone and no matter how exhausted she was she always found herself still thinking about Jake.

She was back to Friday nights being laundry night and she kept things toned down on the weekends. She and Worthless were now the best of friends and together with Alphabet and Shorty they made a fun group. Amanda enjoyed going out to dinner with them on occasion and hanging out at the beach during the day on the weekends. They'd even spent Labor Day weekend in Savannah together.

Her partying days were over though. She'd learned her lessons the hard way again.

Jake's life had also taken a turn. He found himself examining his own goals and asking more questions about what he really wanted out of life. Amanda had made him see that he was becoming increasingly unhappy stuck in limbo as an instructor at the academy. He wanted more out of life and he felt he was finally ready to make some changes.

Amanda was still on his mind a lot. He'd felt something for her that he didn't think came around too often in life, but he also believed that whatever was meant to be would happen. He knew there was still a connection between them because they both watched each other from afar. He was still taking advantage of opportunities to be close to her because he felt he had a certain vested interest in her success here at the academy and in the end he only wanted the best for her.

Much more stressful times at the academy were quickly approaching. After many weeks of training exercises, it was time for the real testing to start. Today, they were finally going to be practicing arrest techniques on role players, who were hired from nearby Brunswick to act the part of criminals. The locals looked forward to these days because it was a good way for them to bring in some extra money.

Adrenaline was running high after the safety briefing and you could almost feel the buzz of anticipation going through the class as the afternoon's events were being outlined.

"Ready for this?" Worthless asked, running to catch up to Amanda as class was dismissed for everyone to reconvene at the site they'd been assigned to.

"Sure. Should be fun." Amanda answered as she and Worthless, assigned to the same team, trekked out to their designated raid house. The raid houses were little bungalows once used for housing, which now served as a kind of stage for various practical exercises. They had everything you would imagine a little house to have. Most had at least two bedrooms and one bathroom with a small kitchen and living room. They were usually sparsely furnished, just to mimic the basics of what you would have to deal with as a criminal investigator in real life if you had to go into someone's house to make an arrest or execute a search warrant.

The raid houses they were going to use today were situated on the outer edge of the academy grounds, over where the townhouse style barracks were that still housed some students. Amanda had a quick recollection of that first night walking back to her barracks with Jake when she'd joked that he might have been agreeing to walk her back to her room way out here. The memory was bittersweet and gave a brief tug on her heartstrings before she mentally pushed all that aside to concentrate on what lay ahead for today.

These practical exercises were designed for the instructors to see how students handled different scenarios, some trained for and some unexpected. It was definitely a lot different than practicing with your fellow classmates all the time.

"Remember to execute this mock raid as though it is the real deal," the instructor for Worthless and Amanda's team of six students said as they were almost ready to begin. They were all lined up, one behind the other for cover as they'd been taught, fake guns out and pointing at the ground.

Worthless and Amanda were the first one's through the door, after the required knock and announce routine. Being first meant it was their job to clear the living room and kitchen as the rest of the team moved on to the back of the house.

"Get your hands up," Worthless yelled at the first role player they came across in the living room.

Amanda headed toward the kitchen to check it for other role players.

"Well, well, well. Must be my lucky day," Amanda heard as she rounded the corner of the kitchen. She stopped dead in her tracks as she saw Tweedledee standing before her.

"Shit," she mumbled under her breath as she pointed her fake gun at him and told him to put his hands up.

Amanda was trying to keep it together, knowing all the while the cameras were on her recording her every move so that her actions could be evaluated later.

"Turn around and face the back wall," Amanda instructed Tweedledee, thinking this could not be happening to her. Of all people to be selected as a role player on this day, why did it have to be the guy whose nose she'd broken in a bar fight?

"I need some back up, " Amanda called out, knowing full well that Worthless had his own hands full handcuffing his suspect. She had a bad feeling about how this was going to go and she just hoped Worthless or another team member would be available to help her soon. Amanda could hear more yelled commands coming from the back of the house and she began to realize that there was probably one role player per team member so that each of them had to perform an arrest. Help wasn't coming soon enough.

Tweedledee had complied with her instructions and now stood with his back to her and his hands up against the wall. Amanda felt she had no choice but to move in and put the handcuffs on. She could hear the whirring sound of the small camera in the kitchen zooming in on her and knew one of the instructors in the control booth was watching closely.

Amanda holstered her fake gun, pulled out her handcuffs and said, "Don't move" to Tweedledee.

Just as she'd gotten one of his wrists in a handcuff, Tweedledee half turned and yanked her around in front of him, pushing her up against the wall. She now had her back to his front and within seconds felt one of his meaty hands grab at her breast while the other went for her gun.

"How do you like me now honey," Tweedledee mumbled sickeningly in her ear. "I've been wanting to get you alone," he said, continuing to fondle her breasts crudely while still trying to take her gun.

All Amanda knew was that he wasn't going to get her gun. She held her elbow down on the hilt of her gun with all her strength and did exactly what she'd been trained to do. She knew this practical exercise was not supposed to get physical like this, but she also knew from the briefing beforehand that the instructors in the control booth would not intervene unless completely necessary. She was also determined not to yell the 'out of role' phrase, which was like tapping out. Instructors used the phrase to signal the end of a scenario. Saying it as a student meant that you couldn't handle your situation and needed help. It was the last phrase any student ever wanted to use. Just like having your gun taken away was the worst thing you could ever let happen.

"Get your hands up now," Worthless yelled from behind them. The back up Amanda had been waiting for had arrived! Amanda quickly took back

151

control of the situation and finished handcuffing Tweedledee.

Unfortunately, she couldn't stuff something into his mouth to keep him from talking. She knew they were all supposed to be trained to ignore whatever might be verbally slung at them, but this guy was really getting to her. He threatened her with various things he'd like to do to her outside the academy gates and ended with how he'd be sure to pick up where he'd left off some other time. He also kept licking his lips in a disturbing manner, turning his head toward her so she couldn't miss it.

"What happened?" Worthless whispered in her ear, coming up behind her as soon as the role player was handcuffed.

Amanda, completely red in the face and sweating profusely at this point, silently turned Tweedledee around, waiting for recognition to dawn on Worthless.

It only took a split second for Worthless to recognize the Neanderthal from the night at the club in Brunswick. Amanda saw his eyebrows go up and his eyes grow round when he fully comprehended the situation. Worthless then quickly grabbed Tweedledee's arm and started escorting him out to the living room, following the rules of procedure established for the mock raid.

"Finally got a little taste of your girl," Tweedledee said to Worthless, attempting to goad him into a volatile reaction.

Worthless could feel his fingers tighten to a death grip on the Neanderthal's arm and had to hear the nasty sound of his laughter taunting him even as he turned him over to someone else and walked away to complete his job during the mock raid. Worthless knew the Neanderthal would be escorted outside by an instructor and then released, this exercise only focused on what happened in the raid house. It was hard to stay in the role he'd been assigned and continue on, making sure the rest of the house was secure. He could only imagine how Harry was feeling.

Amanda was completely shaken at this point, trying hard not to show it. As the mock raid was finally terminated, she stayed behind in one of the bedrooms to try and compose herself before joining everyone out at the front of the house.

"Are you all right?" Jake said, suddenly materializing in front of her.

"Jake?" Amanda said, feeling almost disoriented by his sudden appearance.

"I was one of the instructors in the control booth. We saw what happened initially, but then our view through the camera was blocked by the role player's back when you were pushed up against the wall. We couldn't see exactly what was happening. You didn't call out for help, so we couldn't interrupt the scenario at that point."

Amanda felt herself start trembling ever so slightly, so she sat down on the bed. Jake sat down facing her, taking both of her hands in his, trying to offer some comfort.

"Mandy, tell me what happened. Did that role player hurt you?"

"No. I'm fine. He just caught me off guard," Amanda answered quickly, trying to pull herself together.

"What's got you so upset then? There's something you're not telling me. What did he do when he had you in front of him? Did he assault you?" Jake rapidly fired these questions at her, feeling how cold her hands were in his.

Jake knew something was very wrong here. Amanda was usually so tough and composed, it wasn't like her to let anything rattle her. He suspected there was more to the story than she was telling him, but he didn't know how to get her to talk about it.

Amanda tried again to pull herself together, knowing she couldn't let this incident turn into something worse than it already was. If she told Jake the truth now he'd have to report it. She couldn't let that happen.

"I just want to get out of here now Jake," Amanda said, taking a deep breath.

"Not until you tell me what really happened. That role player will be counseled for not following the guidelines of the exercise, but he won't be dismissed for that. If you tell me he deliberately touched you inappropriately, we can have him arrested and charged. At the very least, it'll go on his record and he will never be hired as a role player here again."

"Are you OK?" Worthless came rushing into the room, asking Amanda. "I was trying to figure out where you'd disappeared to."

Amanda quickly pulled her hands back from Jake's, trying to play things off as though it was nothing out of the ordinary for them to have been sitting on the bed together in the raid house bedroom.

"I'm fine. We were just about to come outside," Amanda answered, starting to get up.

"No we weren't," Jake said, putting a hand on Amanda's leg to get her to stay seated. She jumped up anyway, completely agitated at this point and unable to sit still.

"I'm trying to get some answers here. What the hell is going on?" Jake asked, standing up now too and looking to Worthless for the answers.

"You didn't tell him?" Worthless said in surprise to Amanda.

"Tell me what?" Jake said, as Amanda groaned in frustration at Worthless.

"You've got to tell him what happened Harry," Worthless insisted. "At the very least that Neanderthal deserves to get kicked out of here."

"What's he talking about Amanda? What haven't you told me? Did that role player do something to you?" Jake asked Amanda in rapid succession again. He felt oddly desperate to get to the bottom of what had happened.

Without looking at Jake or Worthless, Amanda simply said, "He just went too far with the exercise. He was trying to take my gun away."

"Are you sure that's all? I told you if he assaulted you we'll have him arrested here and now," Jake said, frustrated beyond belief at this point. His instincts were telling him there was a lot more to the story.

"What do you know about all this?" Jake asked Worthless, putting him on the spot.

Amanda looked pleadingly at Worthless, silently begging him to stay quiet.

"There's more you don't know," Worthless confirmed, while putting his arm around Amanda's shoulders. Amanda tried to stop Worthless from saying any more by turning into his embrace and standing on her tiptoes to fiercely whisper in his ear.

Jake could feel himself tensing up, not only at Worthless touching Amanda so easily and her obviously allowing it right in front of him, but at what he was afraid they were going to tell him.

Worthless shook his head from side to side at Amanda, signaling he wasn't going to listen to her pleas, and continued what he'd started saying to Jake.

"We had an incident with that role player at a club in Brunswick a few weeks ago."

"What?" Jake said, having expected to hear something completely different and therefore not immediately comprehending what Worthless was trying to say.

"She broke his nose and this was probably some form of payback," Worthless continued.

Jake just stared at the two of them for a moment, stunned.

"Obviously if we can keep this between us, Harry and I would appreciate it. We could get in a lot of hot water for not having reported what happened at the time. We never could have foreseen it coming back to haunt us like this," Worthless said, being completely honest, all the while knowing he was asking a lot of Jake.

Jake looked back and forth at the two of them and noticed Amanda still not wanting to make eye contact with him. He couldn't shake the feeling that there was something more to all this.

"I can make sure the role player is dismissed just based on his actions today. What happened between all of you prior to today doesn't have to come into play," Jake assured both Worthless and Amanda.

Turning to Amanda, Jake tried one last time. "Unless he assaulted you. Are you sure nothing more happened in the kitchen when he had you up against the wall?"

Worthless also turned to Amanda, awaiting her answer.

"I'm sure. Can I go now?" Amanda answered, not making eye contact with either one of them.

Jake and Worthless both paused briefly, looking at one another. Then they both shrugged their shoulders, knowing they couldn't do anything if Amanda wouldn't talk.

"Take her back to the barracks," Jake said to Worthless. "I'll clear it with the other instructors."

Worthless thanked Jake.

Amanda remained silent, letting Worthless guide her out of the raid house.

"You know, he's not a bad guy." Worthless said to Amanda as they were making the trek back to their barracks.

"You owe him a great big thank you. Anyone else might not have helped us out of this situation so easily. We both could have ended up in some seriously hot water."

Amanda continued to remain silent.

"Are you OK? Did that Neanderthal do more than you let on? Not that what you described wasn't bad enough already. I wish I could break his nose again." He couldn't help but imagine going another few rounds with the guy.

Worthless was starting to really worry about Amanda when she still remained silent. "Talk to me Harry. What can I do?" Worthless said helplessly, feeling completely out of his element.

Amanda finally took a deep breath and said, "Nothing. I'm fine. Really. He wanted to humiliate me more than anything I think. He didn't get my gun though!" Amanda said, trying desperately to snap herself out of the funk this whole incident had left her in.

"You're a tough one Harry. Don't let this get to you. I got a good look at that Neanderthal's nose today and you really did a number on him. Just put it behind you now," Worthless said, trying to be positive.

"Thanks for coming to my rescue again today. You provided back up just in time," Amanda said sincerely, truly appreciating his friendship and all the times he'd helped her out. "I never would have been able to live it down if he'd gotten my gun from me," Amanda mumbled, knowing that would have made it so much worse for her.

"Don't worry about it. It's over. Besides, that's what friends are for. You and I make a good team! Our stories from our time at the academy alone could rival anyone's now, and it's only half over," Worthless joked, trying to coax a smile out of her.

They finally made it back to the barracks and Worthless was leaving her at the door to her room. "Hang in there and get some rest. It's not every day you get a reprieve around here. Take advantage of it."

Amanda hugged him and mumbled *thanks* as she locked herself in her room.

Amanda had just gotten out of the shower and put on some shorts and a tank top when she heard a knock at the door. She debated not answering when the knocking started up again.

"Can I come in?" Jake asked when Amanda opened the door.

"Of course," Amanda said, knowing she couldn't say no after all he'd done to help.

"How are you?" Jake asked, studying Amanda closely.

"I told you, I'm OK," Amanda said as she turned away to hang up the towel she'd been using to dry her hair with.

"What the...You've got a giant mark below your right elbow already turning into a bruise. Is that from today?" Jake asked, coming up behind her to examine the bruise more closely.

"Yeah, he was trying to get my gun out of its holster, remember, but my training paid off. He didn't succeed," Amanda said with a wan smile.

"I'm really sorry about what happened today. I wish now I would have stopped the exercise," Jake said, silently berating himself.

"You have nothing to be sorry about. You couldn't have known what was really going on and I knew the camera in the corner probably couldn't pick up what was happening," Amanda said, shrugging it off.

"How did you end up in the control booth for my raid house exercise today anyway?" Amanda asked curiously.

"All available instructors have to sign up for the practical exercise days. Since the practical exercises usually coincide with what would normally be your defensive tactics class, you automatically get your defensive tactics instructors thrown in the mix. A list of assignments for the particular exercise is usually printed out beforehand and instructors are given the opportunity to pair up with other instructors of their choice. Thank God, or I'd be stuck with Donovan all the time!" Jake joked, trying to add a little levity to the explanation.

"Anyway, a buddy of mine was already signed up so I simply added my name to his on the list. Later on we get assigned to a particular raid house." He wasn't going to add that he'd looked for her name when the team assignments were finalized, knowing she'd be on the list somewhere. It wasn't a coincidence he'd ended up in the control booth of her raid house.

"Well, I'm lucky you did. You were a godsend today. I know you put yourself on the line for us too."

"I don't know if it helps, but I took care of the creep getting kicked out of the academy for good. He won't be allowed back as a role player again and I made sure he knew to stay far away from you or else."

"Thanks Jake. I'm sorry I didn't say thank you right away today. I really appreciate everything. I know this could have gone a lot differently if anyone else had gotten involved, so I really appreciate your help and your discretion."

"No problem. I just hope Worthless is trustworthy. If any of this comes out later on, I'm risking my job." Jake couldn't help but express his doubts about Worthless again. To be fair, he knew he didn't have an issue with Worthless directly, he just hated how he felt about him always hanging around Amanda.

"I trust him. I wouldn't have let you get put in the middle if I didn't think him trustworthy," Amanda said vehemently, much to Jake's annoyance.

Jake could see how exhausted she was though and decided to let it go at that.

"You look beat. You should probably try and get some rest. I've taken care of excusing you from your last class of the day, so don't worry about anything else today."

Jake went to leave and Amanda found herself wanting him to stay.

"If you need anything, let me know," Jake said as he was opening the door.

"Will you stay with me?" Amanda asked quietly.

"What?" Jake said, turning back to look at her, sure he couldn't have heard her correctly.

"Just for a little while. I really don't want to be alone." Amanda just stood there with her beautiful face looking up at him hopefully.

"Are you sure you don't want to call Worthless instead?" Wanting to kick himself for not being able to stop himself from saying what he'd just said, Jake nonetheless held his breath waiting for her response.

"We're just friends, Jake, nothing more," Amanda said wearily, turning away.

"Promise?" Jake asked quietly, hating that he'd felt jealous and wanting to put it behind him.

"Promise." Amanda turned back to look him in the eye as she said it.

"Let me just make a quick call to get my last class covered," Jake said, locking her door and reaching for his cell phone.

"Oh, I'm sorry. I completely forgot you had to get back." Amanda silently chastised herself for showing such weakness in having asked him to stay with her in the first place.

"I don't. I just have to make a quick call."

Amanda climbed on the bed and got under the covers. Soon Jake was stretched out on top of the covers next to her. Amanda rolled towards him and put her cheek on his chest, snuggling up to his side. Her arm naturally went across his abdomen and met his coming from the other side. Jake lightly stroked her arm with his fingers, more of a soothing gesture than anything else. She realized he made her feel safe. What an amazing feeling that was after the day she'd had. It wasn't long before she dozed off in his arms.

Not much more than an hour later, once the doors started slamming signaling the return of other students to the barracks, Amanda awakened to find herself securely held in Jake's arms, with her cheek still pressed to his chest. He'd apparently fallen asleep as well and was also just starting to wake up.

She put her chin on his chest now and was looking up at him when his eyes opened and focused on her.

"Hi," she said quietly.

"How are you feeling?" Jake said, caressing her cheek with the back of his fingers, thinking he could get used to waking up like this. He loved seeing the freckles on her nose and across her cheekbones. They were only really apparent close up, but in his opinion they added something special to her natural beauty.

"Better. Thanks for staying with me," Amanda said, enjoying his touch.

"Anytime," Jake said, meaning it wholeheartedly.

"You might have to wait awhile until people start leaving for the chow hall if you want to sneak out of here," Amanda said, trying to break the suddenly intimate mood.

"Sure. Will you tell me now exactly what happened with that role player, both today and at the club?" Jake asked, hoping she'd finally talk to him.

Amanda immediately tensed up and said, "I don't want to talk about it." She then pulled away from him to sit up on the bed.

Jake sat up as well, the two of them now facing each other across the twin mattress.

"Mandy, are you sure you're OK? If something more happened, you can tell me. You know you can change your mind and still press charges."

"No. I mean I'm OK, but I'm not going to change my mind about pressing charges. Jake, you know as well as I do that all of this coming out could jeopardize my graduation from the academy. It's not just about me either. This affects Worthless too. I can't jeopardize both of our spots here at the academy and our future careers. At the very least, all this would end up as a blemish on our permanent record. That's no way to start off our careers as special agents. Besides, sometimes things get ugly when you're in this line of work. I'll be more prepared from now on. It was definitely a good lesson in expecting the unexpected."

"He put his hands on you, didn't he Amanda?" Jake asked and Amanda immediately looked away.

"If he did, there should have been more repercussions than just getting fired from being a role player," Jake said in frustration.

"Are you talking to me as an instructor now Jake, or as a friend?" Amanda looked at him inquiringly.

Jake sighed and said, "Whatever you want me to be."

"I really need a friend right now Jake. Can you put your obligations as an instructor aside and just hear what I have to say without thinking you have to do anything about it?" Amanda pleaded earnestly.

"I can try. I care about you Mandy. You know that, right?" Jake said, knowing he'd do anything for her at this point.

Those words warmed Amanda's heart and she realized how much she'd needed to hear that he cared.

"I care about you too Jake," Amanda said in response with a small, sweet smile on her face.

"So tell me what happened. I'll just try and listen." Jake said and watched as Amanda's smile quickly went away and her expression turned serious.

She then started off by talking about the incident in the kitchen at the raid house. "So, you know he could argue that a certain amount of touching went along with the role playing, right?" Jake nodded in agreement.

"Plus, you already said the camera didn't catch what he actually did. So, it would be my word against his and I did break his nose at the club."

"You did, huh?" Jake said, still wondering about the whole story behind that last tidbit of information.

"Yeah, I head butted him!" Amanda said with a laugh.

Jake was happy to hear her laugh. He knew he had a stupid grin on his face at that moment and was reminded once again of how much he loved the sound of her laughter. He also realized how much he'd missed hearing it the past few weeks.

"Well, he grabbed my breasts when he had me up against the wall and his other hand was busy trying to get my gun from me."

The statement came like a punch in the face. He immediately wanted to say something in outrage, but Amanda's hands came up, palms out, signaling him to stop.

"Just listen. I got my butt pinched more times than I can count while I was waitressing to put myself through college. This is similar in a way and I'm not going to let it get to me. Besides, it probably won't be the last time I get groped on the job. It's bound to happen again. It's part of the downside of being a female in law enforcement. Suspects use it to intimidate or humiliate or both. Hell, even some law enforcement officers think they can take liberties sometimes."

Amanda looked pleadingly at Jake. "I can't press charges Jake. It would make all this come to light and I could risk dismissal from the academy."

Jake took a deep breath and tried to remember that he'd promised to listen as a friend.

"Are you sure? He assaulted you. He should be held responsible," Jake said, thinking that even a friend would try one last time to convince her otherwise.

"I'm sure. This is about Worthless too. We'd both have a lot of explaining to do," Amanda said, knowing she was making the right decision.

"What's the deal with you two anyway?" Jake just had to ask.

"Worthless has become a really good friend. He's had my back and I owe him for that."

"Nothing more?" Jake pressed, jealousy rearing its ugly head again.

"I promised, didn't I?" Amanda reminded him.

He nodded in affirmation, feeling bad that he'd even brought it up again.

Then he caught her off guard by asking, "What did Worthless think about you not pressing charges?"

"I didn't tell him everything. He thinks it was all just related to what happened at the club that night, nothing more," Amanda admitted, wanting to be completely honest with Jake.

"Are you sure you don't want to tell him?" Jake asked, trying to be considerate of the friendship she'd mentioned having with the guy.

"I'm sure. He's a good friend and he'd feel obligated to tell me to press charges, despite the consequences to his own future. It's better this way."

"You can still change your mind about this Mandy. It's not too late to report it."

Amanda had already started shaking her head half way through what he was saying.

"I won't change my mind." Amanda said with confidence.

"Still, if you do, all you have to do is come and tell me. I'll help you any way I can," Jake assured her, at the same time trying to respect her decision.

He felt like he'd done all he could. "I better get going now. If anyone sees me now I can still explain it away. Much later than this and it'll be a lot more difficult. Will you be OK? What about food? Should I get something for you?" Jake asked as he was standing at the door, still worried about her.

"I'll be fine. I'm not even hungry. I think I just need to sleep until morning. Thanks again for everything today," Amanda said sincerely.

"Anytime. Good night Mandy."

"Night," Amanda murmured back as he opened the door and left.

As Jake was cutting across the grass, back towards the gym where his car was parked, he got a call on his cell phone from Mark Mitchell, his good buddy out at the Los Angeles Field Office.

"Hey Mark. How are things?" Jake said as he answered the phone.

"Not too bad. Got a minute?" Mark said back.

"Yeah. I could actually use a sounding board myself right about now. Perfect timing," Jake replied.

"Sounds interesting. Me first?" Mark said, eager to ask the question on his mind.

"Go ahead. What's up?" Jake said immediately.

"I just found out I'm getting a new special assignment in about six weeks," Mark started explaining.

"What? You're transferring?" Jake interjected.

"No, nothing like that. It's supposed to become part of my range instructor duties. All I've been told is that there's an injured agent who is transferring to our field office. She was shot in some undercover assignment gone wrong and I've been told she's going to need some extensive rehab time at the range. I was just wondering if you'd heard some scuttlebutt about the incident?" Mark asked, knowing that the academy was a hub for all different kinds of law enforcement information.

"I remember hearing something about an undercover agent being shot not too long ago. It was a pretty big deal, but I don't remember too many details. I can ask around and get back to you," Jake said, racking his brain to remember whom he'd heard it from.

"Thanks, I'd appreciate it. I just want to have an idea of what I'm getting in to. I've never been responsible for something like this and I want to be prepared as much as possible. Everyone around here is being pretty tight lipped about the whole thing."

"So, you're supposed to spend a bunch of time rehabbing this agent on top of all your other responsibilities out there? Weren't you saying a while back that you were shorthanded on help at the range as it is?" Jake asked.

"Yeah, but no one's listening!" Jake could hear Mark laughing at his own joke. He could be such a clown, but he really was a great guy.

"Well, at least this rehab assignment is right up your alley of expertise. You can finally put your education to good use!" Jake said, laughing about the old joke between them. Mark had a bachelor's degree in psychology while most other people in law enforcement had a criminal justice degree. Jake knew this topic always pushed Mark's buttons.

"Very funny. I'm supposed to be rehabbing her shooting skills and brushing up on her reflexes. Nothing to do with her mind," Mark said, only slightly disgruntled by the old joke.

"So much for your psychology degree. Don't kid yourself. Something traumatic like she's been through is going to make getting back in the line of fire pretty difficult," Jake said, needling him on.

"Well, you're just in rare form today, aren't you? I get what you're saying, but I know she's got a department shrink for the psychological stuff." Mark did start thinking that maybe this new assignment wasn't going to be as straightforward as he might have thought at first.

"As for the rest, I know I'll get her squared away," Mark continued, confident in his abilities as a range instructor. "Just try and find out who I am going to be dealing with if you can," Mark reiterated his earlier request.

"Will do," Jake said, thinking he'd probably pushed Mark's buttons enough for one day.

"So, what's your dilemma? Sounds like you have got something on your mind," Mark asked, shifting focus onto Jake.

"I do. Amanda Harrington," Jake said.

There was a short pause and then Mark said, "Amanda from my field office? What about her?" Mark asked, puzzled.

"I'm crazy about her." Jake blurted out.

"What? You're crazy all right." Mark said, starting to laugh uproariously.

"I'm serious, Mark. I can't get her out of my mind and I don't know what to do about it," Jake said, trying to get Mark to understand the seriousness of the matter.

"Jake, she's a great girl, but we're talking about your career here...and hers for that matter.

You can't get involved with a student," Mark said adamantly, realizing this was no laughing matter.

"Too late," Jake said matter-of-factly.

"What the hell's been going on out there? She's only about half way through the academy right now and you're telling me this? You hardly even know her," Mark said, starting to get really worried about what his good friend had gotten himself involved in.

"You said yourself she's a great girl," Jake reminded him.

"Wow, you've got it bad. Sounds like you need a vacation. Georgia must really be getting to you," Mark said, having a hard time believing what he was hearing.

"Seriously, Mark," Jake said, hoping for some honest advice from his friend.

"OK. OK. Amanda is gorgeous. No doubt about that. She's a cool chick to hang around. Even for the short time I've known her, I can easily say so. I may have even thought about going down that road at one point, but even I drew the line at dating someone in the same field office as me," Mark said, leaving out the part that he'd actually pursued Amanda himself initially and she'd turned him down. Now didn't seem the optimum time to mention that.

"That's because you never want a serious relationship. You're mister love 'em and leave 'em. So, you know if you hooked up with someone in the same field office there would be hell to pay once you broke it off. You'd have to see each other day after day and it could get ugly. Don't forget I've known you for a lot of years now," Jake said, being a little harsh with the truth, but wanting to have an honest conversation with his best friend.

"Yeah. You're right about me, but don't forget I know you too. You are probably feeling pretty isolated and lonely right about now. You're almost coming up on two years teaching at the academy and that's a long time for anyone to be stuck in Glynco, Georgia. You might even be feeling downright restless. Lets face it, you haven't mentioned a woman to me in over two years," Mark said, dishing it right back.

"It's different with Amanda though. You're partly right about what you're saying. I have been getting increasingly restless being stuck here. It wasn't like that initially, but it's been feeling like the walls are starting to close in on me here. I want something more than this," Jake said, letting all his frustration out.

"Just don't grab on to the first attractive woman that crosses your path. There are a lot of fish in the sea and it's a big world outside those academy gates. Maybe you need a trip out to California to be reminded of the many available babes I'm talking about?" Mark joked, trying to lighten up the conversation.

"Yeah, right. I know you have a harem out there, but you know I'm a one woman kind of guy."

"Well, Amanda Harrington is not the woman for you. She's a student at the academy you're an instructor at. You need to remember to keep your hands off the students. No exceptions. Students are off limits. You know this."

Jake understood what his good buddy was trying to tell him. It was one thing to think of all this in a clinical fashion in one's brain, but when it came to the heart it was a whole different story. One day Mark would find that out for himself.

"Also think about Timbuktu. Your whole life as you know it would be on the line if anyone found out about you messing around with a student. Even if they just kicked you out of the academy and let you keep your career, your reputation would be in shreds. Then you'd end up in the worst field office imaginable. Remember the joke about agents that get in trouble and get sent to Timbuktu? You have worked way too hard to let that happen. Especially at this point. Once you finish teaching at the academy you can write your own ticket to wherever you want to go. You'll be set. Maybe you should start considering getting out sooner rather than later. Whatever you do, don't blow it all now," Mark said, having given quite the impassioned speech.

Jake remembered thinking those very same thoughts at one point in time.

"I appreciate what you're saying Mark. It's not like I haven't thought about some of that stuff myself already." Jake wasn't sure what he'd been expecting his friend to say about the whole situation. He had probably said what anyone would say who cared about him and wasn't in his shoes. It might even be the same thing he would have said if the situation were reversed. The problem was Mark didn't really understand how strong his feelings were for Amanda already.

"Hang in there." Mark said.

"OK. Thanks for the call. I'll see what I can find out about your new assignment and get back to you," Jake promised.

"Thanks. Just remember my couch is always available!" Mark said, laughing at his own expense.

Jake couldn't help but laugh along with him.

"Later," Mark said before hanging up.

Unfortunately for Amanda, she was still re-playing the events of the day. She'd tried to go back to sleep when Jake left, but she was soon staring at the ceiling. She had to admit she was rattled. It was one thing to put on a brave face in front of the guys and blow off the seriousness of what had occurred. To be true to herself though, she had to admit today had really shaken her confidence. She couldn't get rid of the feeling the lack of control over the situation had given her today. Out in the real world, today's scenario could very well happen again. You were bound to run into people you'd had negative interactions with, especially those you arrested who were once again out on the streets. She knew that. It was all part of being in law enforcement. She had thought she was better prepared. The real problem she was struggling with now was that she could run into these people both on duty and off duty. Off duty there was no back up. No one would be coming to her rescue like they had today. It was a daunting feeling. Her mind was now running to how the scenario might have worked out in the real world. Everything up to and including how he could've gotten her gun and killed her with it. It was all really doing a number on her and for the first time she was really worried about the decision she'd made to go into law enforcement.

Chapter 12

The days at the academy continued with the same routine playing out day after day, regardless of what personal angst one might be dealing with. How well she remembered that from last time. No debacle was going to stop the sand in the hourglass. Between physical training, law classes, shooting range, ethics classes, defensive tactics and whatever else could be crammed in to a day, there was less and less time to think about anything but getting through the days.

It had been almost two weeks since the raid house incident. Amanda and Jake's relationship had changed once again. It felt much more like a friendship, albeit from a distance. They still only saw each other from afar, but their looks now held warmth. Thankfully the days of ignoring one another were over with. Stolen glances were now met with little smiles. Now there was the feeling that they only wanted what was best for the other. Amanda was still sad about what could have been, especially after having it confirmed once again what a great guy Jake really was. She was no longer depressed about it though, because at least now they were back on good terms with one another.

The one thing that had not changed between then and now was the underlying sexual tension that had never gone away and always seemed present when they were in proximity to one another.

Amanda knew she had to stop thinking about Jake and concentrate on what she needed to do to graduate. She needed to stick to her original goals.

All the major testing was now increasing in intensity at the academy. The pressure was on. One big exam after another in every field, back to back. Another student had failed a law exam and had been kicked out of the academy. Two more had failed the qualifications at the shooting range and had been sent back to their field offices in shame. There they would be fired. It was very rare for a student to be "recycled" and given the chance to return to the academy one more time. Usually students were only recycled if it had been for medical reasons that they weren't able to complete the academy the first time around. She'd only heard of that happening once. The bottom line was if you failed anything here at the academy, you could kiss your career in law enforcement good-bye.

Amanda hadn't worried about the law exams or the shooting range qualifications. She knew she was strong in those categories. Today was one of the tests she worried about though. Handcuffing techniques. Today she would have to prove that she could handcuff a suspect successfully and perform a proper search to find any weapons and/or contraband they may have hidden on their bodies. It didn't help that they were bringing in local role players again for the day. The last debacle had shaken her confidence in her own abilities to handle the unexpected. The only good thing was that she knew she'd be handcuffing and searching a female role player. At the academy, handcuffing and subsequent searches for weapons and contraband were only done with the same sex. That's why she and Bulldog had been partnered up for every defensive tactics class involving handcuffing techniques. Now she had to show that she could put what she'd learned in class into action.

"Everyone line up and listen up," Jake said with authority in the hallway outside two adjoining mat rooms at the gym.

"You will each be called into a mat room individually to complete this test. At the end you will be told whether you passed or failed. Remember, the test begins the moment you walk through the door," Jake instructed.

Amanda could feel the heightened buzz of adrenaline from her fellow classmates. Some were antsy and couldn't stand still. Others were unusually quiet and subdued. No one knew in which order they would be called, which only added to the pressure. You were either going to be called immediately or maybe over an hour from now, since each scenario was supposed to last an average of 10 minutes. Both Jake and Donovan, as their defensive tactics instructors, were the final authority on whether they passed or failed.

Jake called out a name for his mat room and Donovan did the same for his. Each mat room also had another defensive tactics instructor that the students didn't know, acting as an impartial witness. This was to prevent students from claiming some sort of prejudice on their defensive tactics instructor's part if they should fail.

Amanda had, of course, known Jake would be here today judging the scenarios. She just hoped she wasn't on the list for his mat room, even though she didn't really want Donovan as her evaluator either. There was just something about having to be tested with Jake watching though, that would make her more nervous than with anyone else.

Almost two hours later, Amanda's name was finally called by Donovan. She'd had a funny feeling after half of the class was already finished, that she just might be last. She had become more and more nervous as the time had ticked by. Sitting in the hallway for that amount of time, going over different scenarios in your head, was sure to psych anyone out. Especially after quite a few people had failed. After the test, each student was allowed to say whether they'd passed or failed, then they had to immediately collect their backpacks from the hallway, put on their shoes and exit the gym. Amanda had watched almost her entire class exit and knew everyone's results. Now it was her turn.

Amanda had failed. She couldn't believe it. When she exited the mat room, there was no one to even say it to, which was probably a good thing. Who wanted to have to announce to everyone that you'd failed? As she was putting on her shoes, Jake came out of his mat room, locking the door behind him. Obviously he'd finished his testing as well.

"How'd you do?" Jake asked Amanda.

"I failed," Amanda replied, avoiding any eye contact with Jake.

"What happened?" Jake asked, wondering what had gone wrong.

"I blew it," Amanda said, disgustedly.

"Which part? Did you miss one of the weapons or a syringe?" Jake just couldn't believe, after watching how well she always did in defensive tactics class, she'd failed.

"No. I blew it right from the beginning. I don't really want to talk about it, OK?" Amanda said agitatedly, trying to get her shoes on as fast as she could.

"Quite a few of your fellow classmates failed today, so don't be too hard on yourself," Jake said, just as Amanda was ready to leave.

Amanda just looked at Jake for a second after that statement and then picked up her backpack to head out the side glass exit door.

"How did it go Harry?" Worthless, Alphabet and Shorty jumped up from being seated against the side of the gym building.

"I failed."

Expletives were quickly heard from all three of the guys.

"What happened?" Shorty asked.

"I'm not really up for a replay right now," Amanda answered, not very nicely.

"Sorry," Shorty said and just kind of hung his head, making Amanda feel bad about snapping at him. She realized no one really knew what to say. Jake had tried too and she hadn't really appreciated the effort.

"Listen guys, I really appreciate you waiting for me. Thanks," Amanda said, knowing she needed to suck it up and have a meltdown about it later.

Worthless just put his arm around Amanda and all of them walked with her toward their last class of the day.

Jake watched all this from where she'd left him standing. For once, he was happy to see Worthless put his arm around Amanda, knowing she was probably already beating herself up about failing. Going last was already difficult and failing on top of it was sure to take its toll. He was actually really happy to see that someone had waited for her. He'd seen too many people walk off alone at the end of the testing. Having some kind of support group was important. Seemed like she'd made some good friends and he was happy for her in that regard.

Later that day, Jake found himself volunteering to be one of the instructors for the handcuffing techniques remedial classes, which all instructors hate doing. That's when he knew he really had it bad where Amanda was concerned. He'd tried to listen to what his best friend Mark had said to him about absolutely not getting involved with a student, but after two weeks of keeping his distance he just couldn't do it anymore. He found himself just wanting to be around her, regardless of the circumstances. He felt like a moth to a flame and realized more and more that he cared less and less whether or not he got burned. There was something about Amanda that stood out and made her different than any other woman he'd ever met. He had to see where their relationship could go, or he felt like he'd regret it forever.

Remedial. Just the word brought with it a bad taste in her mouth as Amanda entered the mat room where the first remedial handcuffing techniques class would be taught. It had been almost a week since she'd failed. There were only going to be two remedial classes before the final retest next week. You either passed then or failed out of the academy.

Nothing like adding an extra hour on to an already long day. By the look of some of the instructors, they felt the same way.

"There are no other females for you to partner with, but I spoke with Donovan and he explained what happened during the test," Jake started off saying, before Amanda had even turned around from taking off her shoes.

She took a moment to compose herself after the shock of hearing Jake's voice behind her.

"Donovan explained that the role player messed up the test scenario. It never should have happened that way and you just didn't react fast enough," Jake continued as Amanda turned to face him.

"However, you completed the search of the role players body correctly and you found all weapons. Therefore, we don't feel you need to be concerned with the search as much as with what happens before the handcuffing. So, we'll just focus on different scenarios that you can complete with a male partner, up to and including the handcuffing. For obvious reasons, you'll skip the physical body search portion," Jake explained matter-of-factly.

"Any questions?" Jake asked, making sure to act professionally as there were many other instructors and students in the room. He had wanted to give her some assurance that she wasn't completely responsible for failing and that she'd done a good job otherwise. He also wanted to quickly explain how the remedial was going to work for her, since he figured it would have been disconcerting for her once she realized she was the only female in the room.

Jake's efforts were completely lost on her at the moment.

Amanda just shook her head no. She was so embarrassed to be in this situation and having Jake there as one of the remediation instructors just made it worse. Now she had to relive her failure in front of him.

Then to make matters even worse, the first guy she was assigned to partner up with had to make a comment about how much it was turning him on to have her handcuffing him. Great.

"Is there a problem here?" Jake asked as he was walking up to them. He'd seen Amanda's partner say something to her that resulted in her turning bright red in embarrassment.

"No," Amanda answered, with her head down.

Jake knew something was wrong, but couldn't do anything about it if Amanda refused to say what the problem was. Instead, he made a point of staying close so he'd be within hearing range if anything else was said.

At the end of the remedial handcuffing techniques class Amanda knew that she'd gained nothing useful from the extra hour. She was already considering skipping the next remedial class all together.

Jake approached her as she was putting her shoes on and said he wanted to speak to her. Amanda tensed up, dreading what he might have to say.

"What happened with the guy you were partnered with today?" Jake asked.

"Other than him getting turned on you mean?" Amanda responded snippily.

"So he said something inappropriate?" Jake responded in concern. "Why didn't you tell me when I asked what was going on?"

"I'm not going to get labeled a rat. Besides, if I got a penny for every time some guy said something inappropriate I'd be well on my way to being a very rich woman," Amanda said nastily, hoping Jake would just drop it.

"I know it must be tough being a woman in law enforcement, but I can't do my part to help if you don't let me," Jake said, understanding where the attitude was coming from this time.

Amanda took a deep breath and reined in her bad attitude, knowing Jake wasn't to blame for anything. She realized she still had some issues left over from what had happened at the raid house with Tweedledee. She better figure out a way to get past them.

"I appreciate your willingness to help, Jake, I really do. I just don't want to make matters any more difficult than they already are. Besides, expecting some guy to practice handcuffing with me without making any comments is probably just too much to ask." Amanda started laughing softly, now finally seeing the humor in it all.

"I'm glad you can find some humor in it. Still, I'd like to be able to help if I can," Jake said, starting to smile now in response to her laughter.

"I think I might skip the next remedial class. Would you be willing to coach me on the possible scenarios that might come up during the retest?" Amanda asked hesitantly.

"Sure. Whatever you need. The remedial classes aren't mandatory, so it's no problem if you miss the next one," Jake said easily, knowing she had the skill set but was lacking in confidence right now.

"Thanks Jake. I'd really appreciate being able just to talk one on one about possible scenarios. I think if I'd been able to think outside the box more, I wouldn't have screwed up," Amanda said, having had a lot of time to think this last week about what had happened.

"Listen, don't beat yourself up about it. You have a week before you have to retest. You'll do fine then." Jake answered.

The mat room had cleared out by now and only Jake and Amanda were left.

"I just can't risk failing. You know I'll get kicked out of the academy if I do," Amanda said, voicing her worst fear.

"Try not to think about that too much. I'll let you in on a little secret. The academy doesn't want to lose good agents on this retest. It's going to be easier than the original test and it's set up for you to be successful. I'll work with you until you're completely confident. You'll be fine," Jake said, trying his best to reassure her.

"Thanks Jake. I really do appreciate it." Amanda really meant it too. Despite everything, Jake was still willing to help her and she was starting to realize that he really was her knight in shining armor. She'd thought he was going to say something negative when he'd asked to speak to her at the end of class, but once again he was putting himself out there for her. She really needed to give herself a break and trust her gut instincts again. Jake really was one of the good guys.

"How about if I call you later to set up a good time for us to meet?" Jake asked.

"Do you still have my cell phone number?" Amanda asked a bit flirtatiously.

"I do." Jake smiled. "I'll talk to you tonight."

Amanda just nodded and smiled back at him as they exited the mat room and went their separate ways.

Later that night Amanda found herself acting like a teenager again, just waiting for a guy to call. It was different this time though. She knew Jake would call. He hadn't let her down yet and she was beginning to realize how much she trusted that he would keep his word.

Sure enough, he called a short time later. They quickly set a time to get together the next evening and then naturally segued into talking about all the things that had been going on since the last time they'd really talked. She was reminded once again how easy it was to talk to him and how they never seemed to run out of things to say or have awkward silences.

"You've got this. You are going to make a great agent," Jake said toward the end of the call, trying to reassure her again about the handcuffing techniques retest.

She realized how much his confidence in her boosted her own. She didn't really have that kind of super positive influence in her life.

"Thanks for believing in me Jake. I'll see you tomorrow."

"Good night Mandy," Jake said softly before hanging up. Amanda went to sleep that night with a smile on her face.

The next night Jake showed up at her room as promised, right after the chow hall closed. She knew it was risky to have him coming to her room, but they'd agreed that she needed all the time she could get for studying this week and any other location was going to take time away from that. Unfortunately, she had another big legal exam at the end of the week and stressing about the handcuffing techniques retest was not helping.

"You know the role player messed up, right? Otherwise you would have passed," Jake mentioned yet again as they were going over scenarios. Amanda knew she was stressed out and it was showing.

"It's just that handcuffing techniques testing has the most potential for the unexpected. I knew that and still had to learn it the hard way. It's the least routine of all the other things we're tested on. Even though it's pass or fail, it's one of the more difficult exams. There are too many variables of what could happen and you really have to think fast on your feet. I just wasn't completely sure what to do, as I'd never even had a scenario like that in practice. This time I want to play out every possible scenario I can think of and have as many answers as possible before I'm put to the test again. In class we've only practiced a few standard scenarios over and over again. That's why when things didn't follow one of those standard scenarios, I froze long enough to cause me to fail."

"The retest will be just the standard scenarios though. I promise," Jake said, trying to do every-thing he could to allay her fears.

"This is about real life though too. I want to be better prepared when I have to handcuff someone later when I'm on the job. I can't afford to freeze and have my mind start racing trying to figure out what to do next. The time I take to think could cost me my life," Amanda said earnestly, wanting Jake to understand how she felt. She couldn't bring herself to tell him these concerns were also related to the incident with Tweedledee.

"I can appreciate that. I just don't want you to keep thinking how every scenario could go horribly wrong," Jake answered, trying to keep her from continuing to stress out over this.

"I can't help it though. My scenario did go horribly wrong!" Amanda exclaimed.

"Yes, but the retest will be simplified and there won't be a margin for any role player errors. I promise. I've seen how the retests are conducted and I know this for a fact," Jake once again tried to reassure her.

"Can we just keep working through different scenarios though?" Amanda pleaded.

"Of course, but can I ask what makes you keep doubting yourself to this degree? You are an exceptional student Mandy. I know for a fact that you've passed all your other tests with flying colors. Your academic scores are always at the top of your class. Don't forget I've seen you at the range too. You're an amazing shot."

Jake really didn't understand this sudden lack of confidence in Amanda, just because there was one thing she all of a sudden wasn't excelling at. Prior to her failing the handcuffing techniques test, she'd always seemed so confident.

"I just can't fail. Failure is not an option." Amanda said wearily, completely exhausted at this point.

It was getting really late and Amanda was so tired. She might not have admitted this otherwise, but she started telling Jake about her family--her dad in particular.

"He just never believed that a girl could be just as good as a boy or even better. He's very old school and believes that there are certain roles for girls in this world and that's it. If I'm honest with myself, I would have to say that I got into this line of work to prove him wrong. You should have seen him when he first saw me in uniform with my gun strapped on!"

"Are you still trying to rebel? Is that why you want to become a special agent now?" Jake asked curiously.

"No. I'm done with trying to prove things to my dad. This is for me. As you know, becoming a special agent will totally advance my career, beyond what I ever could have achieved as an inspector. Also, the pay is a lot better and I have big plans for the future! That being said though, failing out of the academy would still prove to my dad that he was right all along. I can't let that happen."

"What about your mom? How does she feel about all this?" Jake asked, appreciating this insight into Amanda's life. He was finally discovering where the attitude had come from that he'd noticed from the very beginning.

"I would describe her as being cautiously supportive of whatever I want to do. She definitely doesn't like the whole law enforcement thing and I know she worries about my safety. She doesn't really understand what's involved in becoming a special agent--or more accurately, she doesn't want to understand. I've learned not to talk to her about the details of the job and she stays out of the issues my dad and I have with each other. She has definitely had a very traditional role as wife and mother, but she's never made me feel like I have to do the same. I know she doesn't understand my choices sometimes, but at least she applauds my successes and doesn't await my failure like my dad does. Although, if I did fail she might secretly be happy about it. I guess that's why I feel she can't really be 100 percent supportive."

"Does she still call you every day?" Jake asked with a wink, knowing he was thinking of the last time her mother had interrupted them in this very room.

Amanda laughed and answered, "She does. I talked to her earlier as a matter of fact." They both glanced at each other, clearly communicating the same thought. Amanda's mom probably wouldn't call again tonight and therefore wouldn't interrupt anything this time.

The atmosphere in the room suddenly changed dramatically.

"I should get going," Jake said, knowing it was the right thing to do, even after the rather intimate glance they'd just shared. He got up and walked the couple steps to the door.

"Thanks for all your help tonight. I feel better about the retest already." Amanda got up as well and could feel the immediate tension crackling between them as they were facing each other to say good night.

"I'm glad I could help. I'll come by again tomorrow if you want," Jake said with his back to the door, one hand on the door handle.

"I've got that big law exam on Friday, so I'm not sure about tomorrow. I might feel like I better start studying early," Amanda said, trying to think clearly and not let her hormones take over, even though they were clamoring for release.

"How about if I just call you after classes tomorrow and we decide then?" Jake said, trying to stay on his best behavior after having essentially been in her bedroom all evening.

They had both felt the tension building in the last few moments, as it was time to say good night.

"That would be great. Thanks again Jake," Amanda said, standing close to him, not sure why she was testing herself in this manner. She knew they were both trying to behave as friends only, so what was she doing?

Jake knew he should turn and leave, but he couldn't make himself do it.

It seemed they both kind of started leaning in a little toward one another. Once their lips met, the next thing they knew it was like a wildfire raging out of control. They couldn't seem to get enough of each other. They were quickly making up for lost time. Their lips were locked together, tongues dueling, both becoming reacquainted with each others taste. Soon, Jakes hands were fisted in Amanda's hair and she had her arms wrapped tight around his neck. She was trying to press herself as closely as she could up against him. It wasn't long before her body was restlessly squirming against his, searching for just that right fit. Jake felt the same need and finally whipped her around, sandwiching her up against the door. Amanda murmured her approval and started moving her hands up and down his arms, happy to be touching all those wonderful muscles again. Jake started doing the same, moving his hands up and down her sides. They were so tightly sandwiched together that Amanda finally protested that she wanted more access.

"I want to touch you." She mumbled fever-ishly. She'd dreamed about those muscles too often recently to not reacquaint herself with them when given the chance again. She was dying to run her hands over his chest.

In a move that stunned her, Jake reached down, grabbed her behind the thighs and swiftly picked her up as if she weighed nothing. It seemed natural for her legs to automatically wrap themselves around his waist. He then sandwiched their lower halves back against the door and Amanda was immediately rewarded by that feeling of having achieved a near perfect fit. The center of her was now grinding against the hardness of him, giving them both the feeling of pure pleasure their bodies had knowingly been seeking. Jake now leaned slightly back, still maintaining the melding of their lower halves, to allow for the mutual exploration of their upper halves. This is what having all those muscles achieved. Jake was holding Amanda effortlessly and she could only marvel at his strength. Their hands were now moving restlessly over one another. When Jake finally cupped Amanda's breasts in both hands, she knew she cried out in approval. Amanda, leaning forward to give him access to unhook the back of her bra, nipped him on the ear lobe and moved her hands under his shirt to lightly graze his nipples with her finger nails. He groaned and she could have sworn she felt him growing even harder against her. There was now a shared throbbing in their lower regions and mutual titillation ongoing with their upper regions. Jake had pushed up her shirt and bra and was cupping her breasts together, licking from one nipple to the other with his tongue. It felt unbelievably good. Amanda leaned over him, stuck her tongue in his ear and got the reaction she was hoping for. Jake shuddered and groaned in pleasure.

Amanda then whispered in his ear how good it felt to have his mouth on her breasts.

In response, Jake briefly sucked hard on one nipple, making Amanda gasp in shocked delight. Then he went back to licking and nibbling, much to Amanda's pleasure.

Amanda had pulled up Jake's shirt by this point as well and was squeezing and shaping his pecs, then lightly scraping his nipples with her nails.

Amanda felt Jake shudder again at one point as he briefly pulled back and said, "Mandy, you're driving me crazy. Do you know what you're doing to me?"

She gave him a sexy little smile and pulled his head back to her breasts. Jake obliged by lightly biting each nipple and it was now Amanda's turn to shudder in ecstasy. She'd never been this turned on by foreplay before.

They were both driving each other crazy and the wildfire continued to burn.

Suddenly there were voices in the hallway right outside Amanda's door and doors started opening and slamming. All the sounds were like a bucket of cold water. Jake stepped back and Amanda's legs slid to the floor. She leaned her head against his chest, trying to get her breathing under control. Jake put his arms around her loosely and tried to get his raging hormones in check. They both started laughing quietly, but when they finally looked at each other they both quickly leaned in and started kissing again. The wildfire could definitely have kept burning, one bucket of water wasn't going to put it out. However, they both withdrew and knew this wasn't the right time or place to continue this.

Jake took a few deep breaths and pulled down his shirt, while Amanda quickly hooked her bra back into place and pulled her T-shirt down as well. Jake took a few more minutes to try and get his hormones under control, standing with his arms wrapped around Amanda in a warm embrace. She loved the way he held her. Then he gently kissed her on the lips and softly said he'd call her tomorrow. After quickly peeking out the curtains to see if the hallway was clear, he quietly slipped out her door.

Chapter 13

Physical training class first thing the next morning was one of the more interesting classes. Not because of the content, but because of the new awareness Amanda had regarding a certain instructor. After almost going up in flames against the door last night, Amanda found her breasts tingling when Jake would even look her way. The workout was one of the more difficult, but she was sure she had a smile on her face for most of it. Jake sure was pushing the class hard this morning, but he was pushing himself even harder. He kept going during pushups until he'd smoked every last student. Then he did it again with the next exercise. It was like he was issuing a challenge to anyone who wanted to take him on. Some tried, probably thinking that he wouldn't have much left to give, but he just kept going like a machine. Even Donovan was standing back with a smirk on his face, enjoying the show.

Jake was starting to sweat profusely and Amanda became fascinated by how his polo shirt was starting to stick to his chest and arm muscles. She found herself replaying last night and itching to get her hands on that magnificent chest of his again. Last night had been the best foreplay of her life. She'd never experienced those sensations with anyone else. It was blowing her mind to think about how good it could be with Jake and she was having a hard time thinking of anything else.

Granted, she didn't have as much experience as some might think, but she'd messed around enough to know when something was exceptional. Looking over at Jake again, Amanda continued to daydream about just how exceptional he was turning out to be.

Amanda was driving Jake crazy. He was trying not to keep glancing at her, but she had this almost secretive little smile on her lips every time he looked over at her and he'd caught her staring at him several times already. He had a feeling he knew what she was thinking about. Last night had been amazing. She was so incredible and..... He had to stop thinking about last night. He was already killing himself during this workout to keep his body from wanting to react to Amanda simply from looking at her. Besides, she was special and he didn't want their relationship to be just about sex.

She'd really opened up to him last night and he felt he'd gotten to know her on a whole new level. The insight into why she was incredibly confident one moment and then insecure the next gave him an entire new appreciation of what she'd been up against from the beginning. He couldn't imagine having parents that didn't support him 100 percent. He realized that he'd been blessed to have the unconditional love and support that his parents had given him throughout his life, no matter the decisions he'd made.

She was still holding something back. He felt it whenever he tried to touch on her experience the last time she was at the academy. It was a closed subject for her. She shut him down whenever he tried to bring it up. Not rudely, but she quickly changed the subject or immediately said she had to go. She always tried to play it off like it was no big deal, but something had happened the last time she was here and he kept hoping that she would trust him enough to share it with him soon.

As the day wore on, Amanda quickly realized that she better get her head out of the clouds and concentrate. This Friday's big law exam was one of the last critical academic hurdles before graduation. After this week, there would only be two weeks left. In some ways, the time had gone slowly. Now suddenly, however, everything seemed to be rushing by. Most of her classmates had been studying all week in preparation for the law exam and she had yet to start. She promised herself that she would start tackling all her notes tonight. That would mean no spending time with Jake. That was probably for the best anyway. He was distracting her at a time when she needed to concentrate more than ever.

Jake called Amanda later that afternoon, when classes were over for the day, and asked her if she wanted him to come by tonight.

"Not tonight Jake. I've really got to start studying for Friday's exam."

"How about if I just come over for a little while right now, before chow hall?" Jake said cajolingly.

"I'm actually on the look out for Worthless right now. I was hoping to catch a ride to the supermarket before dinner at the chow hall tonight. I need some snacks for my study night, Amanda said a bit self-consciously.

"Why don't I give you a ride to the Piggly Wiggly?" Amanda started laughing as soon as he mentioned the local supermarket.

"I can be there in five minutes. What's so funny?" Jake wanted to know, wondering what he'd said to make her laugh.

"I still can't believe they have a supermarket named the Piggly Wiggly. It just cracks me up every time." Amanda said, still chuckling.

Jake laughed too and said, "Yeah, I remember thinking that when I first moved down here. I guess I've kind of gotten used to it now."

"I can't imagine not finding it hilarious anymore. You've obviously been down here for too long," Amanda concluded.

He'd been thinking that himself lately.

"So, what do you say? Can I give you a ride?" Jake asked again.

She hesitated briefly and then finally admitted, "I'm going to be buying lot's of junk food. You sure you're up for that?" Amanda asked, hoping he wasn't a health food nut.

"Sure, why not? I'll see you in five."

When they pulled into the parking lot of the Piggly Wiggly supermarket, Amanda chuckled once again.

"Seriously, can you imagine a Piggly Wiggly in New York City? I know it would never happen in Southern California!" Amanda said, unable to stop herself from laughing hysterically.

Their banter back and forth about the Piggly Wiggly continued as they crossed the parking lot.

They were both in stitches as they went in the door, hanging onto each other like two little kids sharing a private joke.

"And look, a hippo mixed in with the groceries!" Jake pointed out, laughing even harder.

Amanda looked over and sure enough, there was one stuffed animal sandwiched in between miscellaneous food items on display at the head of the first aisle, right as you walked in the door past the registers.

It was a pretty hilarious sight.

Amanda walked over and picked him up, exclaiming, "He's so cute! This is like the cutest hippo I've ever seen." He had light gray colored fur all over except for the pink on the inside of his little ears and nostrils. His snout was adorably plump and he had little black eyes surrounded by white. He was made to look like he was sitting on his hindquarters with little feet sticking out the sides and at the bottom.

"I wonder what he's doing mixed in with the food?" Amanda looked around to see what display he might have been taken from. There were no other stuffed animals in sight.

"Who knows? Remember, we're in a store called the Piggly Wiggly!" Jake laughed some more, having seen such oddities at this store before.

Amanda started laughing again too.

"OK, Mr. Hippo. Back you go," Amanda said as she put the stuffed animal back where she'd found him.

"You want him, don't you?" Jake asked, thinking how adorable she was, even after having just named and talked to a stuffed animal.

"No," Amanda said, turning slightly red in embarrassment.

"Let's go to the junk food aisle!" Amanda quickly changed the subject, with one last look at the hippo.

"So, what kind of junk food are you looking for?" Jake asked as they started down the cookie aisle.

"Nothing specific. I'll know what I want when I see it," Amanda said perusing what was available.

Jake just stood back and watched her.

"I just need some snacks when I'm studying late at night. You're not going to give me any grief over my choices, are you?" Amanda asked, starting to feel a little self-conscious again, especially with him watching her.

"Why would I do that?" Jake asked curiously.

"I wasn't sure if maybe you were exclusively into protein shakes and health food?" Amanda said, turning towards him with her head slightly tilted, looking up at him inquiringly.

"No way. I mean, I try to eat the right things to help with my workout regimen, but I like junk food as much as the next guy," Jake said, now completely understanding her earlier hesitation about going with him.

"That's a relief. I wasn't sure if I could continue to hang out with you after this or not!" Amanda joked with an impish grin on her face.

Jake loved seeing her in such a great mood.

Pretty soon they had plenty of snacks to get Amanda through the next couple nights and Jake had added a few of his own. They passed the hippo again on the way to the front registers.

"You didn't see a display of stuffed animals anywhere, did you?" Amanda asked Jake, knowing they'd wandered through most of the supermarket together.

"No. Why? Still want the hippo?" Jake asked, winking at Amanda.

Amanda jabbed him in the ribs with her elbow and said, "Isn't it weird that he seems to be the only one in the store?"

"Yeah, I guess that is kind of strange. He was probably just left over from some past display. Or not. This is the Piggly Wiggly after all!" They both started laughing again like little kids.

When they got back out to the car Jake turned to Amanda and said, "I'm just going to drop you off when we get back to your barracks at the academy. I know you need to concentrate on studying for the law exam."

"I do. There's a ton of material to go over and I haven't even started. I'm just going to grab a quick bite at the chow hall and hit the books."

"I know it'll still be daylight when we get back so I was hoping to steal a good night kiss now," Jake said hopefully, leaning toward her with a persuasive smile on his face.

"Please do," Amanda said, blushing as she leaned in the rest of the way.

Jake kissed her softly at first and it was so sweet. Soon it wasn't enough for either of them though and their tongues started dueling. It became awkward with the gearshift between them and they soon came up for air. They were both breathing heavily and when their eyes met they broke out in laughter.

"I can't get enough of you Mandy," Jake said to her, his head resting on the headrest with his arm stretched toward her, the backs of his fingers lightly stroking her cheek.

His touch could be so gentle and loving, Amanda found herself almost wanting to purr like a kitten. Almost.

She still found she couldn't trust her feelings for him completely and pulled away.

"I really need to get back Jake," Amanda said quietly. "Thank you so much for driving me to the supermarket. I really appreciate it."

"Any time," Jake replied, wondering once again about the reason for her withdrawal. It seemed every time they got close to taking things to a whole other level, she put on the brakes.

Amanda aced the exam on Friday and had to admit that she'd really just crammed all her studying into last night. Wednesday night after the Piggly Wiggly had been a complete bust. She'd eaten a bunch of the snack food and had the books open in front of her, but she'd been busy thinking about Jake. She knew she was halfway to being completely in love with him and it scared her so bad.

Then she'd talked to her mom on Thursday night and the topic of her last time at the academy had come up again. It was almost like her mom had a sixth sense about her being involved with someone and felt she had to keep warning her of the mistakes she'd made before. She knew it was because her mom loved her and didn't want to see her hurt again. That didn't make it any easier though.

To top it all off, she was still really worried about her handcuffing retest too. It was coming up on Monday and she'd only had one night so far to go over scenarios with Jake. Unfortunately the last few sleepless nights were catching up to her and she now felt like she was coming down with something.

Jake called after classes were over and congratulated her on her test scores.

"You already heard?" Amanda asked.

"Yes. They tell us immediately, especially when someone fails."

"Just in case they go off the deep end?" Amanda asked half jokingly, half seriously.

"Something like that," Jake replied.

"I can't believe we had two people fail this time. One guy got a 69 and was one point off passing with the minimum required score of 70. Still, we all know close doesn't count. They get to retest on Monday, but one guy also has to do the handcuffing techniques retest the same day. And I thought my Monday was going to be bad."

"You're not still really worried about it are you?" Jake asked.

"I am a little. It's just that whole do or die part of it. Knowing I can be kicked out of the academy, no matter how many other things I've passed successfully," Amanda said worriedly.

"Do you want me to come by tonight and go over some more scenarios with you?" Jake asked.

"Thanks for offering Jake, but not tonight. I'm completely exhausted. It's been a really long day."

"Well, congratulations again on getting one of the top scores in your class. It was probably easy for you, wasn't it?"

"No, it wasn't easy. Luckily I take good notes though!" Amanda said, laughing quietly.

Jake could hear the exhaustion in her voice and said, "How about if I come by sometime tomorrow and we go over some more scenarios until you're completely confident about Monday?"

"I would appreciate that. Let me call you tomorrow afternoon, OK?"

"Sure Mandy. Get some rest."

"Good night," Amanda said, with a smile on her face after he called her Mandy once again. She loved the way he said her name. If he truly knew the power he wielded over her every time he called her Mandy, she'd be in big trouble.

Amanda was able to sleep in late Saturday morning, but woke up with a runny nose, sore throat and other symptoms that signaled that a cold was definitely upon her. She'd been hoping that she was wrong last night and had just been tired, but she felt like crap today and knew she needed to do major damage control to keep it from getting really bad. That meant this weekend was going to suck.

First she took a long hot shower, hoping it would help to clear some of her head congestion. She'd heard Bulldog go out earlier, so she knew she'd be undisturbed and could hog the bathroom. Then she dragged herself over to the all in one convenience store and post office they had here at the academy to see if they had any over the counter cold medicine available. Luckily they did and after grabbing some tissue boxes to go with it, Amanda headed back to her room.

She was completely exhausted again now and after taking some of the cold medicine decided to take a nap. Next thing she knew it was mid afternoon and she was feeling a little bit better. At least the cold medicine had dried up her runny nose a bit so she didn't have to have a tissue glued to her nose the rest of the day.

She knew she needed to call Jake next, but was really dreading it. She still wanted his help running through handcuffing technique retest scenarios, but she didn't want him to see her like this. She also didn't want to risk giving him her cold. She was afraid she was going to be down for the count the whole weekend though.

"Hi Jake, it's Amanda," she croaked into the phone after he answered.

"Wow, you don't sound good at all," Jake couldn't help but comment.

"I've caught a stupid cold," Amanda said miserably.

"That means you need rest, chicken soup and maybe some goodies if you're up for it." Jake rattled this off as if he'd said it a few times in the past.

"Is that what the doctor ordered?" Amanda asked.

"Nope. Mrs. Marshall."

It took Amanda a moment to realize whom he meant.

"Your mom?" Amanda said in surprise.

"Yeah, that's what she'd always say if any of us kids got a cold. Actually, she'd say it to my dad too," Jake said, chuckling.

Amanda had learned so much more about Jake recently. Not only in person, but over the phone. He loved talking about his family and she knew they were all really close.

"Well, I'll get the rest part at least." Amanda said jokingly.

"How about if I bring you the chicken soup and goodies?" Jake offered.

"Depends on the goodies! Just kidding. I'm really not up for anything," Amanda said, her voice sounding terrible.

"I can just come by and drop them off. I don't need to stay," Jake insisted.

"You don't have to do that Jake," Amanda said halfheartedly. Some chicken soup did sound really good.

"I know I don't have to. I want to," Jake said, knowing she probably wouldn't get anything to eat otherwise.

"I just don't want you catching my cold," Amanda said feebly.

"Don't even worry about that. How about if I just drop off some soup? Have you even had anything to eat today?"

Amanda admitted she hadn't and finally agreed to him just dropping off some soup.

True to his word, Jake came by a short time later and handed her a bag through the door, refusing to come in. He said he'd call to check on her later and left. The bag contained chicken soup and some fresh bread to go with it. A giant chocolate chip cookie was also wrapped with a bow in the bottom of the bag. This guy was something else. Amanda had never met anyone like him before. He'd come by without expecting there to be anything in it for him and had brought her food, knowing she wouldn't have gone over to the chow hall tonight. She'd never had anyone take care of her like that, other than her mom, and she hadn't been living at home for a while now.

He did call later and they spent a couple hours on the phone, learning even more about each other's lives and talking about what they saw in their futures. They were surprisingly alike and found many things in common. Jake finally told her to get some rest and said he'd call again tomorrow.

Amanda felt a lot better the next morning. She was still under the weather, but she could tell that staying in most of yesterday had helped tremendously. Jake called shortly before noon and asked if she was up to sharing a couple sandwiches with him. Amanda agreed and quickly jumped in the shower so she'd be ready when he came over.

When Amanda opened the door after Jake's knock she found him standing there with an interesting little smile on his face, a grocery bag in one hand and a sandwich shop bag in the other.

She wasn't quite sure what to make of that smile of his. It was an almost impish, boyish grin.

"What's all this?" Amanda asked.

"Lunch and snacks for later!" Jake answered, still with that grin on his face.

Jake handed her the big paper bag, walking in and closing the door.

He set the sandwich bag on the bed and asked her to get the drinks out of the bag he'd just handed her.

"I see you were back at the Piggly Wiggly?" Amanda said, laughing as she went to set the bag down.

Suddenly she became silent and stood completely still for just a moment. She turned to look back at him and saw him watching her with that little boy grin still on his face.

"I thought Mr. Hippo might cheer you up," Jake said hesitantly, not sure what to think of the way she was looking at him.

Amanda finally just launched herself the few steps it took to cross the room, straight into Jake's arms. He almost staggered backwards from her unexpected exuberant reaction and then just went with it and engulfed her in a bear hug.

She knew without a doubt that she had just fallen completely in love with Jake Marshall.

"I'd kiss you if I didn't still have a sore throat," Amanda mumbled.

"I'm willing to take my chances," Jake said, thrilled by her reaction to his surprise.

She leaned back slightly and looked straight into his eyes, her feet still dangling off the ground. "Thank you Jake. That's one of the nicest things anyone's ever done for me." Then she leaned forward and planted a quick yet soft, sweet kiss on his lips.

It was everything in him not to demand more and lock their lips together for a good long while, but he appreciated the sincerity of her actions and accepted the poignant moment for what it was. He gave her another quick hug and let her body slide down his until her feet touched the ground. That set off some pleasant tingling in both their bodies.

Amanda turned back to the Piggly Wiggly bag and pulled out Mr. Hippo. She hugged the stuffed animal to her chest for a split second and almost wanted to cry she was so happy at this silly yet amazingly sweet gesture from Jake. She quickly reached into the bag and pulled out the drinks and brought them over to the bed.

Jake loved the big grin on her face as she walked over to him, the hippo snug in the crook of one arm.

They spent the rest of the afternoon lounging around her room, which meant either on the bed or on the one chair in the room, and talked about anything and everything. It was amazing that they never ran out of things to talk about and just went from one topic to the next. Before they realized it, it was dinner time. Amanda thought Jake would surely leave now, even though she didn't want him to.

"Are you hungry?" he asked her.

"I am a little," she answered.

"How about we order a pizza?" Jake suggested.

"Sure. Are you sure you still want to hang out though? You don't have to feel like you need to do this," Amanda said hesitantly.

"Haven't we been over this? I want to. I really enjoy spending time with you and I want to maximize the time we have left." It bothered him more and more to think what little time she had left at the academy.

"I'll run out and get some drinks at the vending machine by the laundry room. Do you mind calling to order the pizza?" Jake asked, as he got ready to go.

"Not at all. Which company is it again that's allowed to deliver here at the academy?" Amanda asked.

Jake gave her the information and then quickly kissed her on the lips and headed out the door, saying he'd be right back. Amanda picked up Mr. Hippo and did a little happy dance around the room. Jake really cared about her. For the first time she really believed it with her whole heart.

When Jake walked in with the drinks a while later he said, "I just had a couple close calls."

"What do you mean?" Amanda asked.

"I mean a couple people saw me headed back here, so I changed direction and used the stairs in the middle of the building instead. Then I waited until the people in the parking lot left or went inside. I don't think anyone figured out where I was going, but I think someone on this same floor saw me at your door just now."

"Everyone on this floor, at least on this side of the building, is cool. There are no rats to worry about. I've gotten some light ribbing about you, so if they were going to make trouble they would have already," Amanda assured him. She didn't want to dwell on the potential for trouble right now. She wanted to enjoy Jake's company and not think about what was going on outside her room.

They had a lot of fun eating pizza together and lounging on the bed, squeezed in side by side on the small mattress. Later on they were both seated Indian style, across from each other on the bed. Amanda looked so cute sitting there with the hippo in her lap. She'd been holding onto it for most of the afternoon and evening and she'd thanked him for it several times. They'd been going over scenarios again for her handcuffing techniques retest tomorrow. He knew she was armed with every possible scenario this time and he had no doubt that she'd pass without a hitch.

"You're ready Mandy and you're going to do great." He'd been assuring her throughout the day and she really did feel much more confident now.

"You're going to be there, right?" she asked him.

"Yes. I'll be one of the evaluators. I'll make sure not to get you though. I don't want there to ever be any question about the legitimacy of the test."

"That's probably a good idea," Amanda agreed, thinking of all the things they'd already done that instructors and students were never supposed to do together. All day they'd been dealing with the sexual tension that surrounded them whenever they were together. They'd both been on their best behavior because Amanda still had a cold, but she admitted to herself that she was eager to experience more of what they'd started up against the door this last week. They'd both caught each other eyeing the door at different times throughout the day. It wasn't as if the experience would ever be easily forgotten and the door just seemed to stare you in the face as a constant reminder in the tiny room.

"We'd better call it a night," Jake said, getting up to get ready to leave even though it was only a little after eight. Amanda's mom had just called to check up on her and the call was as much a wet blanket as it had been the first time around.

"That was just my mom calling to wish me good luck tomorrow," Amanda told Jake.

"What about your dad? No good luck wishes from him?" Jake asked curiously.

"My dad doesn't know anything about me failing. I told my mom not to tell him," Amanda admitted. Knowing the family dynamics now, Jake wasn't surprised to hear that. It made him appreciate his parents all the more again. In fact, he was thinking how he should give them a call tonight.

"You should get as much rest as you can tonight and try not to worry about tomorrow," Jake said, figuring she'd probably do the opposite of what he'd just suggested.

"I'll try. Thanks for everything Jake. You've really been the best and I can't tell you how much I appreciate it all."

"How about if you show me with another hug?" Jake said, opening his arms to her. She went into his arms willingly and wrapped her arms around his neck as he picked her up to hug her tight. "That should get me through another day," Jake said with a wink and a smile as he let her body once again slide slowly down the front of his until her feet touched the ground.

Amanda was beginning to think the wonders of a tall, strong, muscular man could be infinite.

They said goodnight and Amanda curled up with Mr. Hippo and had one of the best nights of sleep she'd had in a while.

Chapter 14

It was time for the retest. Amanda had been worrying about it all day, especially after the guy who had failed both the law exam and handcuffing techniques test had flunked his law exam retest this morning. The pressure had gotten to him. Now he was being kicked out of the academy and out of a job. He'd have to find a new career path. That was weighing heavily on Amanda as she waited her turn to take the handcuffing techniques retest.

Jake had been right though. The retest was being handled differently. Multiple students were retesting at the same time and only one mat room was being used. The testing seemed to be going much more rapidly as well, the evaluators quickly cycling through students. Amanda didn't have to wait long at all this time. She'd only seen one other female student waiting to retest and correctly assumed she'd be right after her.

Jake saw Amanda come into the mat room and found himself trying hard not to be distracted from his own evaluation. He just hoped she'd do well and not let nerves get to her. He knew she was pretty cool under pressure most of the time. Over the weekend, she'd admitted it was mostly only on the outside. Inside, she said she was usually quaking. Jake thought it was more of a matter of adrenaline than anything else. Especially before any testing that had serious consequences if you didn't do well, most people would be hard pressed not to be quaking inside. Jake found that Amanda actually under-estimated herself a lot, considering he'd seen her perform under major pressure already and do amazingly well. She put so much pressure on herself to succeed and he understood why. Without someone steadily in her corner since she'd gone into law enforcement, it must have been especially difficult for her. She just needed someone to believe in her 100 percent. Pass or fail. Unconditionally. She was an amazing woman and he was beginning to think that he was just the man to finally give her that unconditional support she needed on a permanent basis.

All of a sudden Amanda hurried out of the mat room. Jake's heart sank. She couldn't have failed already. She'd barely been in the mat room long enough to even begin. Before Jake could even process what might have happened, Amanda came rushing back in. After a brief conversation with her evaluator, Jake saw her actually begin her retest. He put his focus back on the student he was evaluating and said a quick prayer for Amanda to do well.

She'd passed! Amanda was so excited when the evaluator told her she'd executed the handcuffing properly and found all hidden weapons and contraband. Amanda had found a knife rolled into the hem of the female role player's jeans and a syringe hidden in her bra strap. She'd had some sleepless nights over possibly missing a hidden weapon. Especially after finding out that was the reason most other people had failed.

On her way out the mat room door, Amanda glanced over at Jake, hoping he'd look her way for just a moment. Their eyes met briefly and she let the huge happy grin on her face speak for itself. Jake felt such relief seeing that beautiful smile lighting up Amanda's face that he almost felt like a student who had just found out he'd passed as well.

Later as Jake was on his way to pick up Amanda, he realized how connected he felt to her on every level. Her stress and agony this last week had weighed heavily on him and today her success felt like his as well. He realized how much she had come to mean to him already and how invested he felt in her doing well. He truly wanted only the best for her, always. Tonight, it just seemed natural to want to celebrate her success with her. He was happy she'd felt the same way. She had said yes immediately to going out to celebrate, when he'd called her right after he evaluated the last student retest.

They celebrated with a seafood dinner at a restaurant on St. Simon's Island. The conversation was at times light and at other times more serious, but always positive, focusing on the future. Jake knew their relationship had gone to a new level over the past week, but there was one topic that seemed to be a dark cloud over them. Jake needed to know that Amanda trusted him enough to finally share what she'd been holding back. Something had happened her last time at the academy that had put up walls around her. He felt like the walls were cracking, but without a bulldozer he didn't think the walls would come down in time to put their relationship on an even deeper level. Jake was coming to realize that he saw his future with Amanda in it. He just needed her to see it as well.

The problem now was time. They were simply running out of time. The academy was almost at an end and Jake decided it was now or never. He wanted to ask Amanda again about what had happened the last time she'd been at the academy. He felt if he was right about it being significant, they could put it behind them once and for all and move on. He knew the best was yet to come if they could jump this last hurdle together.

So, Jake prepared to be the bulldozer.

"How about if we park at the beach for a while and talk?" Jake asked Amanda as they were driving away from the restaurant.

"Sure," Amanda answered.

They parked in the almost empty lot next to the pier on St. Simon's island and rolled down the windows, letting the warm breezes blow through the car. Thankfully, it was a mildly humid evening. The sound of the waves gently lapping the shore was soothing and Amanda and Jake sat quietly for a few moments simply enjoying the peace and quiet.

"There's something I really want to talk to you about," Jake said, turning sideways in the driver's seat to face Amanda.

"So, you really did bring me here to talk?" Amanda teased, laughing softly as she turned toward Jake.

"I did," Jake said quietly and Amanda now picked up on the seriousness of his tone and expression.

Jake was really nervous, wondering if it was a good idea to try and make this conversation happen now. Then he thought about how they had so little time left and he had all this hope for the future....

"I really care about you Mandy. You know that right?" Jake reached out and took Amanda's hands in his.

Amanda just nodded her head affirmatively, wondering where this conversation was going.

"I'm hoping that we've built enough trust now in one another that you feel like you can talk to me about anything."

Amanda's stomach started to clench.

"Whenever we've tried to make real strides forward, there always seems to be something holding you back. I'm hoping we can talk about it, put whatever it is behind us and give ourselves a real chance at a relationship."

Dread was sitting like a rock in Amanda's stomach now. Amanda turned away from Jake, pulling her hands from his grasp. She then sat facing forward in the passenger seat, with her arms crossed in front of her chest.

"You know I won't judge whatever happened, right? It's in the past. I want to leave it there and move forward. With you."

Amanda continued to sit in silence, staring out the front window at the water, her stomach churning horribly now.

"Am I wrong in thinking that there's something that happened the last time you were at the academy that's keeping us from being able to move forward?"

Amanda shook her head no and finally said, "You're not wrong Jake. I just haven't been able to bring myself to talk to you about it."

"Please talk to me now," Jake pleaded.

Amanda stared out the front window a while longer, battling with herself internally over how to explain things to Jake. She knew she needed to learn to trust her instincts again. She'd done a lot of soul searching since being back at the academy. If she was truly honest with herself, she could now admit that she'd turned off her sixth sense the last time she'd been at the academy. Then when things had gone horribly wrong she had blamed her instincts, when she'd ignored them all along. There'd been signs she just hadn't wanted to see. Looking back on it all, they had been right there in front of her face.

She felt like she had no blinders on this time and was seeing things clearly. She trusted Jake. He'd been nothing but good to her. He deserved the truth. She'd made a big mistake and had paid for it heavily. It was time to forgive herself and move on.

Amanda looked over at Jake just sitting there patiently, waiting for her to explain. She felt love for him well up inside her. She knew no matter what happened, she'd always remember Jake fondly. She was going to trust herself this time and go with what she truly felt in her heart. Whatever time they had left she was going to make the most of. This conversation was hopefully going to put the past behind her. Then she'd take all the memories they'd made from this time at the academy, finally let them wipe out the old bad memories, and bottle them up to hold on to when her time at the academy was over.

"My first time at the academy seems like forever ago now. I was young and naive. Even though we're only talking about a year ago, it seems like another lifetime to me. Turns out I lead a pretty sheltered life. Mostly saw the good in people. Worked my way through college with no real time for a social life. Didn't date much. Never had a serious boyfriend."

Amanda realized she was starting to talk in choppy sentences and took a deep breath to pull herself together. Jake nodded, seeing Amanda needed some encouragement to continue. They'd talked extensively about their lives recently so Jake understood a lot of what she was explaining now.

"When I first got to the academy as an inspector I got more attention from guys than I'd ever had the whole rest of my life combined. I was always the pretty girl that never got asked out because guys assumed I was already taken or stuck up. At the academy, it was all suddenly different. There was a constant parade of guys asking me out and it was flattering at first, albeit very overwhelming. I admit I flirted outrageously at the beginning and really had fun just joking around, not taking anything or anyone seriously. I was never mean spirited about it though. I simply never agreed to a date with anyone and treated all the guys pretty much the same. I thought all the flirting was quite innocent, since I had no intention of getting involved with anyone."

Amanda was speaking in this monotone voice now, which really bothered Jake. He could tell it was her way of trying not to let any emotions from the past affect her now.

"There was one guy though. He's an inspector with our agency, out of the New York Field Office. He was so charming and always seemed to know just the right thing to say. I didn't take him seriously at first, but he was very persistent. He pursued me more than any other guy there and we started spending a lot more time together. I started to believe that he really did care about me and that he wanted a future together and not just a fling. He even talked about plans to transfer to my field office so we could be together."

Amanda's hands were clenched together in her lap now.

"I gave him my virginity. Turns out he was trying to win a bet," Amanda said, deadpan.

"WHAT?" Jake said, stunned.

"Two inspectors from my field office, that I'd become friends with, came to me the morning after and told me about the trash talk in the locker room. They apologized for not saying anything sooner and said something about not wanting to be rats and break the guy code. Anyway, apparently they'd heard the guy collecting on his bets that morning and couldn't in good conscience stay quiet any longer."

"Son of a bitch," Jake blurted out.

"Yeah. It gets better," Amanda took another deep breath before continuing. "Turns out all the guys I'd supposedly turned down decided to gang up on me after that and started saying crude things to my face. I got propositioned a lot too."

Jake watched her hands clench and unclench, seeing how difficult it was for her to talk about it all.

"The worst was what happened at my field office. All kinds of stories made there way through the gossip mill once I got back. So, this one big mistake became something that I couldn't escape from. I was labeled as easy and suddenly went from being a virgin to being thought of as a whore."

Amanda gulped in some air again finally, having sped through trying to get it all out.

"Anyway, hopefully you can see now why my mom is so overprotective of me. I cried on her shoulder for weeks afterward. When she found out I was going back to the academy again, she made me promise not to make the same mistake twice."

"Guess you haven't told her about me?" Jake said jokingly, trying to lighten things up a little.

"Nope."

"So, that's why her call was like a bucket of ice water thrown on us that first night in your room?" Jake said, basically having asked a rhetorical question.

"Yeah. All makes sense now, huh?" Amanda said with a wan smile.

"It's starting to." He now had all the pieces to the puzzle and was looking back on everything they'd been through together in a new light.

"I'm sorry Mandy. I'm sorry you had to go through that. I'm sorry you met some asshole who couldn't see the treasure he had right in front of him."

Now it was Jake's turn to take a deep breath.

"I'm not that guy though. It's different with us, you know that right?" Even as he was saying it he felt like a jerk. He thought about how hard it must be for her to believe him. It did really all make sense now. That asshole must have fed her all kinds of lines. He wouldn't be able to prove to her that he was one of the good guys with words. He'd have to show her with actions.

"I'm learning to trust my instincts again. I do believe it's different with us. I also understand the academy is a place in time and I just want to make the most of the time we have left," Amanda said.

"It doesn't have to be over at the end of the academy Mandy. We can..."

Amanda put her fingers over Jake's lips and said, "Let's not dwell on the end before we have to."

Jake understood all too clearly once again that words were never going to be enough. Everything he said now seemed like a line after what she'd just shared with him. After all, she'd heard them before and had ended up hurt.

"Thanks for listening and not judging," Amanda said quietly, sincerely thankful to him.

"There was nothing to judge. You trusted the wrong guy and you paid heavily for it. Unfortunately, I see academy flings happening all the time. I myself have become quite cynical about people's behavior in general around here. I think that's why you stood out so much to me this time around. I could see all the attention you were getting when you first got here, but you ignored it all."

"Yes. This time I wanted to make sure I didn't mistakenly encourage anyone," Amanda said ruefully.

"You know, I've seen even the most unattractive girl get a lot of attention here at the academy. It's the oddest phenomenon. Too many men and so few women. Rules seem to go out the window when everyone gets here," Jake said, thinking back to all he'd seen during his times at the academy.

"So, how are things at your new field office?" Jake asked curiously.

"Fine. Although, speaking of my field office, it sure threw me for another loop when I found out how close you and Mark were," Amanda admitted.

"Yeah, I can see how it would have. You've probably been worried all along about more stories getting back to your field office. You're not still worried are you?" Jake asked.

"No. I know you talk to Mark. You've been open about your close friendship with him and I would have heard something by now if he'd blabbed," Amanda joked, at the same time knowing she was half serious.

"Mark's one of the good guys. He might be quite a player when it comes to the ladies, but deep down he's got a heart of gold. He would never discuss anything I've shared with him in confidence. I trust him completely," Jake assured her.

Something else about her story had been bothering him.

"So, this guy was from the New York Field Office too?" Jake asked, thinking of all things for him to have in common with the guy.

Amanda just nodded in affirmation.

"Another horrible coincidence," Jake mumbled, shaking his head at the irony of it.

"Yes. It seemed like that should just be another warning for me to stay away from you," Amanda said, remembering what it had felt like when Jake had mentioned where he was from.

"Didn't work out that way though, did it." Jake couldn't help but grin at this point.

"Hardly. It seemed like I just kept running into you and it got to the point where I couldn't get you off my mind," Amanda grumbled good naturedly.

"The feeling is mutual, although I was partly responsible for the amount of times we were put together. I've already come clean on that, though, haven't I?" Jake laughed as he reminded her.

"Yes. You have! I'm flattered by it now. Don't worry." Amanda thought back to the past weekend when Jake had openly admitted to trying to spend as much time with her as possible. She knew now, just as she'd suspected at the time, that he'd deliberately filled in as an instructor when he'd known it was for her or her class.

Jake was worried though. He realized that it was a miracle that they'd come as far as they had in their relationship. With all she had trusted him enough to reveal this evening, he could see the eerie similarities she'd been fighting against all along when it came to him and this other guy.

"What was the guy's name anyway?" Jake had to ask.

"Oh Jake. I'd rather not say. There's no point in it, is there?" Amanda said, exhausted now after telling Jake everything. What she really wanted now was to never discuss any of it ever again.

There was to him. He'd like to kick the guy's ass if he ever got the chance.

"Not right now anyway," Jake finally said and let it go for now.

"How about a short walk on the beach before we head back?" Jake suggested.

"I'd love that," Amanda said with a smile.

They held hands and just walked along the shoreline in silence, enjoying the moonlit night. Each of them seemed preoccupied with their own thoughts, but there was a definite new closeness between them that was palpable.

At one point, Jake just turned to Amanda and took her in his arms, holding her as they both stared out at the ocean. It was a wonderful embrace. Sweet and gentle. There was something pure about it that offered reassurance that what they had together really was a good thing. Amanda finally let herself truly relax into Jake's embrace and just enjoy the moment. For the first time she felt like she could really put the past behind her and move on.

Jake felt Amanda relax against him and they stood hugging one another for a long time. Finally, he pulled back slightly, cupped her face in his hands and kissed her. It was an undemanding kiss full of genuine affection, with just a hint of the fire that always seemed to be there between them when they touched. For tonight, it was the perfect way to end the evening.

Chapter 15

It was the last Friday night at the academy. This time next week she'd be on a plane headed home. She didn't want to dwell on that tonight. Another long week was behind her and Amanda was looking forward to seeing Jake tonight. They had talked every night this week, but because of two more exams, now passed and thankfully behind her, they hadn't seen each other since their celebration dinner Monday night.

"I want to take you to this special little beach I go to sometimes. It'll be deserted at this time of night and we can have it to ourselves," Jake said, after they'd had a nice dinner at an out of the way diner.

"Sounds good," Amanda said, wanting to spend as much time with him as possible.

The beach was on the quieter side of St. Simon's island, away from the pier where everyone else would be flocking to. Amanda could tell it was a beach that most people probably wouldn't even know about because it seemed as if Jake had pulled off the road in the middle of nowhere. Thankfully the moon was almost full, lighting up the night just enough for them to be able to see their surroundings.

"This time we're not here to talk!" Jake said with a wink and a smile. He grabbed a blanket out of the back of the car and took her hand, pulling her down a small trail toward the beach.

Amanda simply laughed and went along on the adventure. The trail was only wide enough for one person and the vegetation was pretty thick on either side. If Jake hadn't kept hold of her hand as she followed behind him she probably would have found the whole experience unsettling.

Amanda realized she was finally at the point where she had truly come to trust Jake. She knew she would go wherever he led her. She was living in the moment and felt happy for the first time in a long time. Happy to be with this great guy who cared about her and who she knew she was in love with. She was going to make the most of the time they had left together with no regrets. No more worrying about tomorrow. She was going to take this happy feeling and bottle it up to treasure later.

She was almost jittery knowing the step she wanted to take with Jake tonight. The one thing she was sure of was that she wanted her memory bottle to be full of the good stuff.

Jake had no agenda for tonight. He loved spending time with Amanda and wanted to have as much of it as he could get. He especially loved hearing her laugh as she trailed behind him down to the beach. He was quickly coming to realize that whenever he thought about her, or spent time with her, or talked to her for hours on the phone, he always used the word love to describe it. That had never happened before. He'd never met someone that he loved everything about--until now. He knew he was in love with Amanda. Really in love. He found himself wanting to tell her, but was afraid of what she'd think. Given recent revelations about what had happened to her at the academy the last time, he was treading carefully.

When they came out of the almost stifling vegetation onto the beach, it was such a relief. Then Amanda took in the scenery that had been revealed and simply stared in awe. They were now on a short stretch of beachfront with the waves gently lapping at the shore.

"Wow. How did you ever find this place?" Amanda asked, soaking everything in.

"It's another local hideaway. Not too many people know about it. I had to promise to only share it with someone special," Jake said, immediately hoping that hadn't sounded like too much of a line. He was speaking from the heart, never having brought another woman here. The problem was, did she know that? He found himself scrutinizing everything he said to her lately, not wanting to appear at all similar to that asshole from her past.

"I'm honored. It is absolutely beautiful," Amanda responded, appreciating her surroundings and not reading anything into what he'd said, taking it at face value the way it had been meant.

"Come on! Let's find a spot to spread the blanket on the beach," Jake said, feeling really happy to be there with her. He needed to stop thinking about what she'd told him about her last time at the academy. He was over thinking everything he said to her and it was still coming out wrong. He needed to go back to being himself.

They walked a little further down the beach and spread the blanket on the sand. Jake then took Amanda in his arms and simply held her for a time, both of them staring out at the ocean.

"I missed you this week," Jake whispered softly.

"I missed you too," Amanda whispered back, lifting her head to stare up into his face.

Jake's hands then came up to cup her face and he slowly lowered his lips toward hers. Anticipation hummed through Amanda. She wanted his kisses and so much more. She sensed that he was trying to keep his libido in check, but she wanted him to stop treating her with kid gloves and really make her feel like the woman that had finally emerged once she had left the past behind. Jake had been so much more careful with her since she'd told him what had happened in the past. She appreciated that about him, but at the same time she had finally put the past behind her and wanted to move on. She wanted the Jake back that was the strong, virile man she'd fallen in love with. That man made her finally feel like a woman.

The woman inside her definitely thought it was time to come out and play!

So, Amanda took the initiative and quickly turned Jake's sweet, gentle kiss into a raging inferno of heat. She gripped the back of his head with her hands and pulled his lips tightly against her own. Then she slipped her tongue into his mouth and started exploring. She instantly felt the change in him. His arms tightened around her and he groaned into her mouth, deepening the kiss even more as his own tongue joined in. His hands then roamed her back, first tangling in her hair and then moving all the way down to caress her bottom. He molded his frame to hers and they were pressed up against one another as tightly as possible. Amanda then tried to tug him down to lie on the blanket. Jake released her mouth and seemed to be taking in huge gulps of air.

"We need to slow down Mandy."

"No, we don't," Amanda said heatedly, trying to get him to continue what they'd started.

"We do. I want you so much I can barely contain myself. That kiss of yours just shot my temperature up to the boiling point," Jake said, putting his forehead on her shoulder and breathing in the wonderful scent that was uniquely hers.

"I want to be with you Jake," Amanda said softly.

"Oh Mandy. I want to be with you too. But, I want to make sure you're really ready for this step."

"I am. I'm so ready," Amanda promised.

"Are you sure?"

"Yes, Jake. I couldn't be more sure."

Jake looked deep into her eyes and saw the sparkle in them reflecting back at him. She was so beautiful. He wanted her desperately, but was still concerned he might be lumped in with the memories of her past. He knew this was very different for him, but he still wasn't sure about where he fit in with her.

"No regrets," Amanda whispered, looking up at Jake. She could see he was still hesitating and she loved him for that all the more. It was further proof of how much he cared about her and she knew making love with Jake would never be a mistake. What other guy that she had ever known would hesitate once given a green light?

Amanda took Jake's hand and pulled him down on the blanket next to her. They started kissing again slowly, but the raging inferno was back again in no time. Their chemistry together was so hot, it amazed Amanda that they'd restrained themselves so long.

Jake was burning up, realizing that his fantasies were about to come true. He was finally going to make love to Amanda. He wanted to go slow, to make sure she realized how much he cherished her. She seemed to have other ideas though. She was touching him everywhere now and even started removing his clothes. He tried to get her to slow down, but she was having none of it. It really turned him on to see this more aggressive side of her, yet he realized it had been there all along. She'd just been afraid of letting it loose. After all, she was a federal agent and could kick ass with the best of them. He loved seeing the strong woman he knew her to be, coming out full force. Wow. When she decided to go for it, there was no holding back!

Amanda loved having her hands all over Jake's muscles again, skin to skin. He was a beautifully built man. She couldn't seem to get enough of touching him. Jake was now working on removing her own clothing and she found she didn't have a care in the world about where they were or what was going to happen here. She loved this man and for her, tonight was going to be a culmination of all the feelings she had for him.

As soon as Jake had her shirt and bra off, he simply took a few seconds to stare at the wonder before him. Here was Amanda, spread out on the blanket with the moonlight shining on her perfect breasts. He knew it was a sight he'd never forget. His hands were then quickly cupping her breasts and his fingers began pinching her nipples until they were hard as erasers. Amanda moaned and started arching her back up toward him, begging for more. Jake lowered his head and started licking and sucking on one nipple, while still tweaking the other. Amanda thought she'd come apart right then. What he was doing with his hands and mouth was incredible. She now had her hands linked behind his head, holding him close and found herself squirming for release.

Jake then kissed his way down her stomach and started unfastening her shorts.

"Red panties, my favorite!" Jake said, glancing up at her with a quick smile and then kissing her intimately through the thong underwear. His mouth followed the slow removal of her underwear and shorts, leaving tiny kisses all the way down her legs. As soon as she was free of her clothing, Amanda decided to turn the tables on Jake.

"My turn," Amanda said with a sexy smile as she pushed Jake onto his back. His shirt had already been removed earlier, so Amanda went to work on his shorts. She could now see the bulge behind his zipper and lightly caressed it, cupping him intimately. Jake groaned and said, "I love your touch, Mandy, but I have to warn you. I can't take too much of that or this will be over rather quickly."

Amanda just gave him a sexy little smile and started lowering his zipper. There was a definite tent in his underwear now and Amanda removed his shorts to reveal his own sexy undergarment.

"Love these," Amanda exclaimed as she caressed his thighs through the boxer brief. She loved this kind of underwear on men. Super sexy.

Everything about Jake was just perfect for her. She realized that she couldn't have dreamed up a more perfect guy for herself.

Jake couldn't take much more and flipped Amanda back over onto her back to finish getting naked himself.

"Hey, I wasn't finished! No fair!" Amanda exclaimed, laughing happily. She was now almost giddy with anticipation.

"I was going to be finished pretty quickly if I'd let you continue, if you know what I mean," Jake said as he reached for his wallet in the back pocket of his shorts. Thankfully he always carried an emergency condom in his wallet, as most boys were taught from an early age.

Amanda blushed scarlet red, watching him sheath himself, but she couldn't look away.

Jake looked up and saw she'd been watching him and gave her a knowing wink and smile as he now moved into position between her legs. He started kissing her again and she felt like this moment was her own small slice of heaven.

His weight pinning her down.

The blood coursing through her veins as if she'd had a straight shot of adrenaline.

His amazing touch.

The anticipation of what was to come.

Jake slowly started moving to achieve that ultimate, perfect fit. He kept on kissing her, his tongue now starting to mimic what his body wanted to do, going deep into her mouth, withdrawing, then dipping in again. Amanda felt a gentle nudge between her thighs and spread her legs, hooking her ankles around his back to let him know she was willing and ready.

He entered her slowly, carefully, still kissing her passionately. It was everything in him to restrain himself, but he wanted so badly to make this first time with Amanda the best it could be.

Amanda was in heaven and felt eager for more. She felt like her whole body was wrapped around him at this point, her arms and legs pulling him as tightly to her as possible.

Once he was completely inside her, he paused for a moment to ask if she was OK. She could see the sweat beading on his face and realized what his restraint was costing him. She nodded and assured him she was ready for more by tightening her ankles around his back and lifting herself even deeper into his embrace.

Jake groaned loudly and finally started thrusting in and out of her, faster and faster. He knew he was close to the edge and wanted Amanda to go over the edge with him. So, he levered himself up on his hands and leaned in to suck hard on each of her nipples, almost sending Amanda over the edge. The final moment came when he eased a hand between them to finger Amanda most intimately. She exploded and took him with her.

They curled up in each other's arms afterward and simply enjoyed the beauty of their surroundings. Amanda felt the wonder of being in a special place spiritually, that she'd never achieved before and possible never would again with anyone else. She knew she needed an emotional connection with someone before sharing a physical connection and Jake was only the second man she'd ever been with. If it was up to her, he'd also be the last. She also knew life didn't always work out the way you hoped and she needed to stick with enjoying the moment and not thinking about the future.

Jake was ecstatic. Being with Amanda was better than he'd even imagined it could be. He felt his body starting to respond again and picked up Amanda's arm to start kissing her hand, then her wrist and up her arm. Amanda smiled lazily at the romance of it and dreamed a little dream of what it would be like to have this amazing man in her life for always.

Jake then kissed Amanda on the lips and what started as a sweetly romantic gesture quickly turned hot again.

"Come back to my place with me," Jake whispered.

"Let's just stay here a while longer," Amanda said back, not wanting to leave yet.

"I only had the one condom with me. I want you again, so much, but I want to protect you. Let's go back to my house. It's a short drive from here," Jake pleaded.

Amanda wanted to be with him again too.

"OK. I'd love to see your place," Amanda said, giving in easily. She quickly started searching for her clothes.

"Well, it's temporary as you know. It's been a great rental since I've been here though. You'll see," Jake said, happy that she'd agreed to go with him.

They quickly dressed and made the short trek back to the car. The trail, which had seemed almost creepy at the beginning, now became an almost magical element to the whole evening. Amanda realized that they'd had what had seemed like their own isolated island for a short magical moment in time. Looking back from the side of the road, she never would have guessed at the beauty that was just beyond the weeds. She locked the memory of the evening deep in her heart as she got in the car. When she'd thought about wanting to have some good stuff to fill her memory bottle with, little did she know that the reality of it all would be beyond her wildest dreams.

Jake's small bungalow was only a short drive away. It was almost hidden at the edge of the marsh, tall vegetation and clever landscaping blocking the other houses in the neighborhood from having a view of one another. It was very rustic on the inside, sparsely yet comfortably furnished. It was also surprisingly neat for a bachelor pad. She had expected more of a mess, especially considering he couldn't have known they'd end up back here tonight.

"This is my home sweet temporary home," Jake joked, referring to what Amanda had similarly once called her barracks at the academy.

"I can see why you like it out here. Must be nice to get away from the academy to a place like this at the end of the day," Amanda said, looking around.

"It is a really relaxing, quiet place. It's also close enough to everything that I don't feel like I'm way out in the middle of nowhere. When I first saw it, I knew it was perfect. It's only one bedroom, but it does have a king sized bed, which really sealed the deal for me. What more do I need right now?"

The place just had a good feel to it. The small kitchen had everything necessary and was open to a decent sized living room. A short hall with two doors on either side of it, one to a bedroom and one to a bathroom, finished the place off.

"I got a great deal on the rent, as the owners usually only get renters for the summer and love having someone year round. So, I've been able to build quite a nest egg in the almost two years I've been down here," Jake went on to say.

Amanda appreciated that about Jake. He seemed frugal and often talked about his plans for the future. She didn't see him blowing money like a lot of other students and instructors were known to do while at the academy. This proved once again that they really did have a lot of things in common.

"Are you hungry at all?" Jake asked, knowing he himself was hungry, but not for food.

"Not really," Amanda answered absently, still taking everything in, enjoying the personal touches he'd added to the place. It was fun to see the picture of him with his family on the coffee table. Finally she was able to put some faces to the names of the people he talked so much about.

"Why don't I show you the rest of the place then?" Jake asked, leaning against the counter in the kitchen with his ankles crossed, in what Amanda thought of as his sexy pose. He had a big grin on his face and Amanda couldn't help but smile back.

"Lead the way," Amanda responded, letting the happiness just bubble up inside her and leaving the worries behind.

By the time they took the few short steps to the ajar bedroom door, Amanda was already back in Jake's arms and they were kissing as if it was going to be their first time all over again. They started ripping each other's clothes off and were naked and on the bed in record time.

Jake initially came down on top of Amanda on the bed, but she soon pushed him onto his back and quickly straddled him.

"I believe my turn was terminated early last time," she said as she began licking his nipples.

Jake half laughed and half moaned at this unexpected turn of events. He loved her spontaneity, which he'd only caught glimpses of up until now.

"Mandy," Jake groaned loudly as Amanda lightly bit one nipple. "I still can't take too much of this, you know," Jake said, breathing hard.

One of her hands traced the line of hair down his stomach and soon encircled the part of him that most longed for her touch. Jake's whole body jerked when Amanda started stroking him. He quickly had to stop her hand, telling her that he was too close to the edge. In one motion, he flipped Amanda onto her back and quickly reached into his nightstand for a condom.

Amanda laughed softly at the urgency of his actions, but was quickly moaning in ecstasy when Jake's hand found her wet and ready for him. He entered her swiftly and they raced over the edge together.

Amanda spent the rest of the weekend, holed up in what she thought of as their love nest. It was so quiet and peaceful, something she hadn't been able to appreciate for many long weeks now. They slept, made love, slept some more. They ate whenever they were hungry and even showered in the bathroom's tiny shower stall, plastered together so they could both fit. Amanda spent most of the weekend either naked or wearing one of Jake's shirts, oddly unconcerned about her lack of personal toiletries and attire. Jake never failed to tell her regularly how much he loved her natural beauty. So, she just went with it and relaxed completely, enjoying the weekend for what it was.

Jake went out for groceries at some point, but other than that they existed in their own little world. The time of day seemed insignificant and Amanda knew she would have some of the most incredible memories to put in her memory bottle. On Sunday evening, when she knew it would soon be time for her to go back to the academy, she was lying next to Jake in bed, studying his body so she could commit it all to memory.

"Have I mentioned how nice it is that you keep yourself all trimmed up?" Amanda teased.

Jake laughed and said, "I believe you mentioned that at some point when you were getting a close-up!"

Amanda blushed and said, "Well, it's worth mentioning again!"

Jake just smiled and wondered how, after the marathon weekend of making love and becoming as intimate as any two people can get, Amanda could still be blushing. He loved that about her though. She was such a unique woman. Shy one minute and a wildcat the next. Jake loved everything about her.

He'd tried several times over the past two days to put their conversations on a more serious note, but Amanda always interjected something about just living in the moment and enjoying the time they had together. It worried him a little, but he knew they still had time and he didn't want to rush her.

"I've got to get back to the academy Jake," Amanda said finally. He'd been trying to convince her to spend the night, but she didn't want to have to wake up super early and risk being seen with him in the morning. It was a little easier to take the risk under the cover of darkness, which nighttime obviously provided.

When they were ready to go, Jake stopped her at the front door and gave her a steamy kiss.

"I'll miss you tonight," Jake murmured in her ear, sending goose bumps up and down her body.

"Ditto," Amanda said, trying not to get emotional. She hated long drawn out scenes. She'd been dreading this moment all day, but knew it had to arrive and now she just wanted to get it over with.

Jake sensed Amanda's withdrawal and didn't press her on the silent drive back to the academy. Outside her barracks, she gave him a quick kiss before quickly getting out of the car. He barely had time to say that he'd call her tomorrow.

Amanda was in turmoil when she got to her room. It had been such an amazing weekend with Jake. Leaving him had been gut wrenching though. Their time had been so idyllic and now the end of it all was closing in. She thought she'd be able to handle it better than this, but it was already taking its toll.

The phone in her room started ringing as she was just about to get into bed. She had a feeling she knew who it was.

"Hello Mother," Amanda said as soon as she confirmed the identity of her caller. She then had to make up a story about celebrating with her classmates on their last weekend at the academy. What threw her for a loop was the question about why her cell phone was going straight to voice mail since Saturday night. Amanda checked her purse and realized her phone battery was dead because she hadn't thought about it once the whole weekend. She told her mother she'd just forgotten to charge it. Her mom was a smart lady though and knew something was up. She also knew her daughter well enough to know that she wouldn't get anything out of her if she didn't want to talk.

After hanging up with her disappointed mom, who probably suspected there was a guy involved again, Amanda crawled under the covers of the bed and stared up at the ceiling for a while. She hated not telling her mom the truth, but she herself hadn't yet wrapped her head around everything that had happened. It was simply too soon to talk about it all. Amanda said a quick prayer that she'd be able to handle what was to come at the end of the week and soon fell into a deep, exhausted sleep.

Chapter 16

The rest of the week took on an almost unreal quality. Amanda made the decision Monday morning to jam her memory bottle as full as she could get it. She was in love with Jake and wanted to spend as much time as she had left with him. As soon as classes were over, she and Jake headed out to his rental house on St. Simon's island and spent the evening together. They cooked up a quick dinner together and spend the rest of the time in bed making love. One or two nights they even skipped dinner and went right to bed! It was as if they both felt the short amount of time they had together coming to an end and they wanted to fill it with as much time together as they could. Late every night Jake would drive Amanda back to the barracks, never able to convince her to spend the night. He knew she wasn't a morning person and getting up even earlier to get back to the academy before everyone started waking up wasn't going to work for her. So, he complied with her wishes, happy that they spent every evening together, but missing her sleeping beside him through the night.

On Thursday, the night before her class graduated from the academy, Amanda suddenly said no to coming out to his house for the evening. Jake was surprised, as he had planned a bit of a celebration for her. He'd even taken part of the day off to get everything ready, pretending to have a doctor's appointment so he could get a couple hours off.

"I'm exhausted and I haven't packed up anything yet. You know I won't have time to do it tomorrow," Amanda explained quietly to Jake on the phone.

Worthless was in Amanda's room at the moment, the two of them wanting to say their good bye's to one another. Amanda motioned to Worthless that she'd be just a minute. Worthless winked at her with a smirk on his face, probably guessing whom she was talking to.

"It's our last night together though. I wanted it to be special," Jake said cajolingly.

Amanda turned away from Worthless and started whispering, "All our nights have been special. I've loved every minute. I'm just worn out and I can't make the drive back here late tonight and still pack everything up. I'd be barely conscious tomorrow if I did that. Then I have a long flight home..."

Amanda wanted to start crying. She was feeling close to her breaking point. She was emotionally, physically and mentally drained. All the late nights and lack of sleep were taking their toll again.

"Why are you whispering? Is someone there with you?" Jake asked, suspicious as to why she was acting this way.

"Yes. Worthless and I were just doing some reminiscing on our last night here." Amanda turned back in time to see Worthless flop onto her bed, his hands behind his head, staring up at the ceiling as though he knew it was going to take longer than a minute for her to end this call.

"I'll get you back early tonight," Jake promised, refraining from making some comment about Worthless.

"I know you mean that now, but we said that on several of the other nights too. Instead it kept getting later and later. You know when I'm with you I don't want to leave." Amanda didn't want to have a contentious last phone call with Jake at this point, so she was saying more in front of Worthless than she probably would have normally. She knew even with the quietest whisper possible, in a room as small as this one was, Worthless could probably still hear everything.

Looking over at him and judging by the even bigger smirk on his face, she knew he'd heard every word. Worthless sat up and motioned that he would leave. Amanda shook her head no and motioned for him to stay put. He flopped backwards on the bed again.

"I should go. Can we talk about this later?" Amanda said, wanting to end the call and not have any more of this conversation with Worthless in the room.

"Mandy, please let me spend some time with you on your last night. I'll come to your room if you don't want to come to the house. Just for a little while," Jake pleaded.

Amanda couldn't say no. She wanted desperately to see Jake on her last night, she just didn't know if she could handle it emotionally.

"OK," Amanda sighed into the phone, giving in.

"OK? Great. I'll be there in about an hour. Can you get rid of Worthless by then?" Jake grumbled.

Amanda let out a chuckle and said, "I'll try."

As she hung up the phone, Worthless sat up and said, "So that's where you've been the last week? I should have guessed."

Amanda shrugged and felt herself turning a telltale shade of red.

"He's a good guy, you know. You could do worse," Worthless said matter-of-factly.

"Wow. This coming from you?" Amanda said in surprise.

"I gotta tell it like I see it. He helped you out on more than one occasion, especially when you could've gotten in a lot of trouble. Hell. He helped me out too. He could've turned us both in, but he didn't. He put his job--no, his career--on the line for you every time he helped. A guy like that doesn't do that for just anybody. He obviously cares about you." Worthless said in all seriousness.

"I care about him too. I just got in way over my head," Amanda said, feeling completely drained.

"Something tells me, so did he. What are you going to do about it?" Worthless asked, curious about what she had planned.

"What's there to do? We graduate tomorrow and I'm on the first plane home," Amanda shrugged, trying to dismiss the question.

"That doesn't have to be the end of everything," Worthless said, knowing what he'd said earlier was true. No way did a guy do everything Jake had done for Amanda and then just walk away when her time at the academy was over.

"Sure it does. How many long distance relationships do you know of that work?" Amanda said with a forced laugh.

"Don't ask me, I can't even make the short distance one's work!" Worthless joked.

"So what...you're the romantic all of a sudden?" Amanda said in irritation.

"Maybe. I've just gotten to know you pretty well these last few months and I don't think you'd jump into a relationship with just anyone at this point. Obviously you saw something special in Jake, otherwise you wouldn't have given him the time of day and you would have treated him like you did the rest of us poor slobs."

Amanda looked at Worthless closely after that statement.

He just shrugged and said, "I know you just saw me as a friend from the beginning, so I went with it."

"Why didn't you ever say anything?" Amanda asked.

"Would it have changed anything?" Worthless said, already knowing the answer.

"Honestly?" Amanda hedged.

"No. Lie to me," Worthless said with a smirk.

"Probably not," Amanda finally admitted.

"I knew that. Deep down I knew the answer. Once I saw you with *our instructor* that night on the pier, I knew I didn't have a chance anyway! Now, I've come to really appreciate our friendship. I hope we can stay friends and keep in touch. Besides, there's someone out there for everyone, right? Now I just need to find my someone."

"What makes you think I've found mine?" Amanda questioned, reading into what Worthless had just said.

"Just a hunch," Worthless said with a wink.

Amanda quickly dismissed his hunch and said, "We'll absolutely stay in touch. You never know. Maybe we'll work on some cases in each other's backyards every once in a while. Other than that, Southern California is a great vacation desti- nation. You'll always have a free place to crash."

"I'll keep that in mind," Worthless said, meaning it.

Worthless and Amanda hugged each other good-bye, knowing there'd probably be no time for them to interact privately tomorrow.

Amanda had just finished packing her big suitcase when there was a knock at her door. She knew it had to be Jake and she took a deep breath before opening the door.

"Surprise!" Jake said, from behind a balloon bouquet.

After a moment of shock, Amanda quickly pulled him inside her room.

"What are you doing? Did anyone see you? Are you crazy?" All came out jumbled together as Amanda stood looking at him.

"I had these for you at the house, but since you wouldn't see them there, I had to bring them to you."

"Oh Jake. It's a wonderful surprise. Thank you." Amanda smiled, looking at the mix of Mylar and regular helium inflated balloons. One balloon said "Congrats" and another said "Way to go." It was a large colorful display and Amanda's heart melted at the sweet gesture.

"This is for you too," Jake said, handing her the box that was in his other hand.

It had a bakery label on it and Amanda set it on the desk to take a peek. Inside was a small heart shaped cake with blue icing on it that read, "Congrats Special Agent!"

Amanda barely held back the tears as she went to give Jake a big hug. He let go of the balloons and wrapped both his arms around her. Amanda laughed as the balloons hit the ceiling. Then she planted a long kiss on Jake's lips.

"Thank you. I had no idea you had this planned. I'm sorry I didn't come out to the house," Amanda said, feeling really bad now about having said no to going to his place tonight.

"I wanted to surprise you, so I guess I still managed that," Jake said, content now that he was holding her in his arms.

"You did. It's a wonderful surprise. Thank you," she said again, reaching up with her hands to pull his face down for another kiss.

"You're welcome. I'm so proud of you. Congratulations on finishing the academy and becoming a Special Agent!"

"I can't believe it's actually over and we graduate tomorrow," Amanda said, pulling out of his arms now and heading back toward the cake.

"Want some?" Amanda asked as she was opening the bakery box.

"Absolutely. Let's celebrate!"

There were two forks in the box with the cake so they both grabbed one and reached in for a bite.

"Yum. This is delicious," Amanda mumbled around a mouthful of cake.

"Yes it is," Jake said in total agreement. They both reached into the box for seconds, laughing as their forks bumped one another.

They briefly discussed the graduation ceremony that was going to take place tomorrow. Jake said he'd be there. Then they started kissing and the next thing they knew, they were naked on the bed after an energetic bout of lovemaking.

Amanda sat up after a while and smacked him on the shoulder saying, "I knew this would happen. I haven't even finished packing." Now she found herself feeling exhausted physically, yet wired mentally.

Jake tried to pull her back to spooning with him, but she jumped out of bed agitated. He smiled, watching her walk around naked, looking for the clothes they'd haphazardly discarded earlier. She caught him watching her unabashedly and started turning bright red. She then tried to get dressed quickly, all the while pretending as if it was no big deal being naked in front of him. She'd been naked in front of him plenty of times in the last week, but she still couldn't help feeling self-conscious with him staring at her like that.

Jake finally gave her a break and sat up to get dressed himself. Now it was Amanda's turn to enjoy what she saw, although she was less blatant about it.

Jake helped Amanda pack up the last few things, other than what she'd need to get ready in the morning.

"What about Mr. Hippo?" Jake asked, holding him up with a grin.

Amanda grinned back and said, "Leave him out. I want to pack him last tomorrow morning." She wasn't going to tell him that she was actually planning on packing him in her carry on. Mr. Hippo was precious cargo and she wasn't going to risk him disappearing due to an airline baggage mistake. Also, she didn't want him becoming deformed beyond recognition on the flight home, which she knew would happen if she crammed him in her suitcase. Mr. Hippo was going to be her special reminder of their time together.

"It's getting late. I better get going," Jake said, knowing he'd promised to only stay for a little while.

Amanda just stared at Jake for a second or two and then slowly walked up to him and said, "Stay."

"Are you sure?" Jake asked in surprise.

"Yes. Stay with me tonight. You can get up early in the morning before anyone else, right?" Amanda said, teasing him about what he'd tried to convince her to do before.

Jake laughed. He thought quickly and said, "Yes, I can just get up and go and take a shower at the gym. I always keep an extra set of gym clothes in my office just in case, so it's no problem."

"Great. Time for bed," Amanda said with a seductive smile on her face as she came up to Jake and started pushing his shirt up to help undress him.

Jake pulled his shirt off and started helping Amanda with hers. She'd left her bra off when she'd gotten dressed earlier and her breasts had been tempting him, jiggling around unbound. He'd been half hard since they'd gotten out of bed earlier and it didn't take much to have him standing at full attention again. Just the sight of her beautiful lush breasts was enough.

Amanda noticed the big bulge in his pants right away and smiled knowingly, happy that they both couldn't seem to get enough of each other. They quickly undressed the rest of the way and this time Amanda pulled a condom out of her nightstand for Jake.

"I just figured I'd be prepared," Amanda said in answer to Jake's look of surprise.

"Good thing you are, since I already used the one I had on me," Jake said thankfully, realizing it hadn't dawned on him that he wouldn't have had a second condom.

"Allow me," Amanda said as she unwrapped the condom and covered him.

Jake could still barely contain himself when she touched him intimately. She seemed to have this innate knowledge of exactly how to touch him. He'd never known anyone who could generate all these feelings inside him time and time again. It was more than just sex. He knew it was love this time around. He wanted to tell her, finally.

Jake entered her slowly and paused when he was fully inside her. He stared at her face, waiting for her to open her eyes. She did, wondering why he'd stopped. They stared into each other's eyes and Jake said, "I love you Mandy."

He saw tears quickly start to sparkle in her eyes as she said, "I love you too Jake."

Then he began to move in and out of her slowly, relishing every moment. Soon, going slow wasn't enough for either of them and Amanda pushed him onto his back and straddled him. Jake reached up and cupped both her breasts, tweaking her nipples as Amanda rode him. When he knew he was close, he reached down to rub her where they were joined and it sent her over the edge, once again taking him with her.

Amanda collapsed on top of him, completely spent. The last bit of energy she hadn't even known she still had was gone. Jake caressed her back for a bit and then turned on his side, allowing Amanda to gently slide off of him. She then turned her back to his front and the two of them fell asleep, spooning one another, one of Jake's arms around her waist and his hand cupping her breast.

Jake woke up very early at the first sign of light coming in through the cheap curtains on the window, disoriented at first until he realized he was in Amanda's barracks room. She was curled up against his side, both of them having spent the entire night attached because there wasn't enough room in the twin bed to sleep apart.

Jake had to admit there was something to be said for a small bed every once in a while!

Jake knew he should get up, but couldn't resist staying in bed a little longer. He was happy just holding Amanda in his arms. Another thing he'd never felt before with anyone else. He thought back to the night before and immediately wanted to repeat it all again. Amanda had been completely exhausted though. He wanted to wake her, but at the same time he knew she had a long day ahead of her and needed all the sleep she could get.

As difficult as it was, Jake made himself get up out of the bed and get dressed. Before leaving the room, he leaned over the bed and gave Amanda a soft kiss on her cheek. She mumbled something in her sleep, but didn't wake up. Jake smiled, knowing he'd see her later and would hopefully be able to reveal everything to her then. With one last look at her, he quietly let himself out of her room.

Amanda woke up to the sound of doors banging shut and voices in the hallway outside her window. She stretched for a moment, smiling at her memories of last night, before quickly turning toward the clock to see what time it was and coming fully awake with a start. She quickly looked around and realized Jake was already gone. She couldn't believe she'd slept through him leaving! At least he hadn't overslept too. She'd never set her alarm and now she was going to be late for her own graduation. Plus, today was the day she had to get all dressed up and wear a suit instead of her uniform. She'd planned on spending a little extra time on her hair, but at this point she'd be lucky if she got the bare minimum done.

At least there was no time to think.

Amanda made it to the graduation ceremony, with no time to spare. She'd quickly clipped her hair up and thankfully her suit had been pressed and ready to go before Jake's visit last night. She'd caught a ride over with another classmate who'd been running late and had finished putting on her make up in the car. Turned out they were flying out of the same airport later today and he'd offered her a ride if she could get her stuff together right after the graduation ceremony. She quickly said yes to the offer, not having relished the thought of having to take the shuttle bus to the airport. Worthless was flying out of the Glynco airport along with Alphabet and Shorty. Unfortunately for her, her field office had booked her return flight out of Jacksonville, Florida. The flights were direct from there to the west coast, but the drive time to the airport was a lot longer.

Throughout the ceremony, Amanda kept looking for Jake but couldn't see him anywhere. There was a small crowd, some families having traveled to the academy to watch the graduation. Just like last time, Amanda had told her parents not to bother. She knew the ceremony would be short and that flights from the west coast were expensive. She always wondered if her dad would even have bothered to come, but once again decided it wasn't really worth it to have that question answered.

After the ceremony, Amanda took another quick look around for Jake. He'd said he would be there and she couldn't believe he hadn't come. She was almost numb at the thought that this was how it was going to end with them. Her ride was ready to go though and they quickly drove back to the barracks. She had no time to waste thinking about anything. She quickly threw the last of her things together and went to put them in the car. Before she knew it, they were speeding down to the airport in Florida.

Everything had gone wrong for Jake already that day, from the moment he'd left Amanda's room. Before he'd even had a chance to take a shower at the gym, he'd been stopped by one of the head instructors and was told he'd have to fill in for someone who'd called in sick. He'd then tried to call in every favor he had to get someone else to cover for him, knowing that otherwise he'd have to miss Amanda's graduation. He finally got someone to fill in for one of the classes, so at least he could say good-bye to her before she got on the shuttle bus to the airport.

He'd planned on surprising her with a ride to the airport, after he'd watched her graduate, but so far nothing had gone as planned. Now here he was at the shuttle departure lot trying to look inconspicuous and she was nowhere to be found. He'd stopped by her room beforehand, but there'd been no answer and it looked as though she'd already cleared out. He'd tried to call her cell phone, but it was going straight to voicemail. He saw a couple other people from her class, but didn't want to ask them about her. He knew from his conversation with her last night that she'd planned on catching this shuttle today, so where was she?

Amanda was already sitting in the airport terminal awaiting her plane's departure, which was still a couple hours away. She'd jumped at the chance to get a ride to the airport instead of having to take the shuttle, even knowing that she'd have some time to kill once she got here. After she'd seen Jake's name come across on her cell phone's caller identification a couple times, she'd finally just turned it off. She didn't know what had happened today, but the last thing she wanted was a lame good-bye over the phone. She was barely keeping it together as it was. She didn't want to start crying over the phone and blubbering something stupid. She still had a long travel day ahead of her and she couldn't afford to fall apart now.

It was time to go home and put everything else behind her. She'd successfully graduated and achieved her goal. She'd become a special agent. She finally had the career she'd always wanted. Now she could move forward with all the plans she'd made for the future. She should have been thrilled.

Instead, she felt awful and couldn't wait for the day to be over.

Chapter 17

Six weeks and counting. Amanda couldn't believe it had been six weeks since she'd graduated from the academy and she still couldn't get Jake Marshall out of her head. She was beginning to think she was never going to be able to move on from him. It seemed like she thought about him every minute of every day. She should be thinking of him less and less, instead it seemed to be the opposite. She couldn't help wondering if he'd moved on himself or if he still thought of her...

Sure, he'd tried to stay in touch with her at the beginning. He'd call and leave messages or send e-mails and texts. She just hadn't seen the point in any of it. Their situation wasn't going to change and she didn't want to go down a dead end road, prolonging the misery of what was sure to be the horrible demise of their relationship. Plus, she couldn't stomach the thought of him cheating on her, which was eventually going to happen, right? Didn't everyone always say long distance relationships were doomed?

So, here she was at work, accomplishing exactly nothing. She was sitting behind the desk in her office with the door closed, staring out the window at the cars going by on the freeway the office building overlooked. She knew her mood was dark and her pessimism about life in general was taking over. It was her own fault she'd cut off all communication with Jake. She'd thought it was better to just rip off the bandage and end things rather than peel the bandage off slowly knowing the eventual outcome. Besides, she knew she couldn't just be friends with him after everything.

Someone knocked on her office door and Amanda made sure it looked like she'd been working before calling out,

"Come in."

At first she felt like she must be hallucinating. Stunned, Amanda could only stare at the person who had just come in, closed the door, and was now leaning up against the back of her office door.

She felt momentarily frozen in place, as if someone had used a stun gun on her and she couldn't move.

"Hello Mandy," Jake said softly, enjoying the shocked look on her face. He himself felt unable to move, joy and fear both warring inside him now that this moment was finally here. There was the joy he felt in his heart at finally seeing her again, drinking in everything about her. Then there was the fear of the moment of truth finally being upon him. He wondered if everything he'd done to get him here to this moment in time was going to be worth it in the end.

"Jake?" Amanda said in awe, yet with a question mark, not fully believing that he was really standing here in front of her. "What are you doing here?" She asked in wonder.

"Well, you stopped answering my calls or responding to my e-mails," Jake said matter-of-factly.

"I was trying not to postpone the inevitable," Amanda said back, snapping herself out of the daze his sudden appearance had put her in.

"Why does it have to be that way?" Jake questioned quietly.

"It was going to be too complicated," Amanda answered, trying to remember all the reasons why.

"So, you didn't even want to try?" Jake asked, looking at her intently.

"I couldn't see the point. What was going to change?" Amanda said, growing increasingly uncomfortable under his scrutiny. It was such a shock seeing him here in her office, she wasn't sure what to do. One part of her wanted to run into his arms and kiss him senseless. Her common sense on the other hand, kept telling her that wasn't a good idea and his sudden appearance didn't necessarily mean that anything had changed. She still didn't want a long distance relationship.

"Have your feelings changed?" Jake asked, watching her closely as he started moving toward her.

Amanda started rearranging the piles of paperwork on her desk, not wanting to answer the question.

"Did you miss me these last six weeks?" Jake asked, now standing in front of her desk, looking down at her.

Amanda felt paralyzed, not sure how she should respond. He still hadn't said anything about why he was even here.

"Mandy?" he questioned her again softly.

Oh how she loved when he said her name like that.

"What do you want me to say? What's the point of all this?" Amanda blurted out, suddenly exasperated. She was afraid to give in to the feelings at war inside her. She jumped up in agitation, her chair hitting the wall behind her as she faced him across her desk. "Why are you here?" She finally asked the question she really wanted an answer to.

Just looking at him made her weak in the knees. She should have remained seated.

Jake glanced at her desk and sure enough, there was Mr. Hippo in the corner by her computer, just as Mark had told him he had been since the day she'd returned to work after the academy. Jake reached over and plucked him off her desk, holding the hippo in front of him.

"Did you miss me?" Jake asked again, making the hippo kind of dance in front of him, taunting her deliberately. He now had that adorable boyish grin on his face and Amanda couldn't help melting on the spot.

"OK...stop. Maybe just a little," Amanda said, his antics with Mr. Hippo making her start to laugh.

"So, that's a yes?" Jake asked as he now came around her desk to stand directly in front of her.

Amanda looked up at him and saw the huge smile on his face, his eyes exuding the warmth and love she had come to cherish her last week at the academy. It was all still there.

"Yes!" Amanda laughed and closed the distance between them, wrapping her arms around his neck as he bent to give her the kiss he'd been dying to give her the moment he walked in the door. The kiss quickly turned heated and they were both breathing hard when they pulled back, reigning in their feelings in deference to the fact that they were in her office at work.

Jake cupped Amanda's face the way she loved and tilted it toward his so he could look deep in her eyes.

"I love you," Jake said, loud and clear.

"I love you too," Amanda responded in kind, without hesitation.

Jake then shocked Amanda even more than she thought possible by getting down on one knee and pulling a small jewelry box out of his jacket pocket.

"Will you marry me?" Jake asked, opening the box simultaneously and revealing a sparkling diamond solitaire engagement ring, which he held out toward her.

"What? How are we possibly...? Oh Jake," Amanda said, alternately staring at him and then at the ring. She was so completely stunned at this point she wasn't sure how to respond. So many things were going through her head.

"Mandy. Answer me with your heart. We can work out all the other things your head is asking later."

That made it easy. Jake was right. There was only one answer to give. Without further hesitation Amanda gave her answer. "Yes. YES! I'll marry you," Amanda exclaimed, her heart feeling like it would burst.

Jake jumped up and they simultaneously wrapped their arms around one another, kissing and laughing and both talking a mile a minute.

"First things first," Jake said as he took the ring out of the box and put it on her finger. Amanda just stared at it in delight. Then she threw her arms around Jake's neck again and started kissing him like she never wanted to stop.

"Mandy. We can't do this here," Jake started saying after some very intense kissing and intimate touching, both trying to get reacquainted again quickly. It was everything in him to stay sane and try and slow things down.

"We have to stop," Jake mumbled again between kisses, wishing they didn't have to.

Amanda couldn't get enough of him. She still could hardly believe he was here in the flesh. She couldn't have dreamed of a better moment and she didn't want it to end.

"I want to clear everything off this desk and take you here and now, but we have to remember where we are," Jake said, wanting to give in but knowing he couldn't. She was tempting him beyond belief. It had been so long since he'd held her, kissed her, been deep inside her.

"You don't even have a lock on the door," Jake finally mumbled in frustration, knowing that if anyone walked in on them right now they would already be found in a compromising position. Amanda was sitting on the edge of her desk and Jake was standing between her open thighs with her legs wrapped around him.

Amanda laughed and said, "Funny that you noticed that right away!" She slowly started coming to her senses. She knew Jake was right and this wasn't the time or place.

"Of course, I wanted to get my hands on you as soon as possible, preferably without interruptions," Jake admitted, knowing a lock on the door might have changed things!

Amanda hugged him tight, still not quite believing that this was all happening. She finally stood up and straightened her clothing, trying to cool down her overheated libido. Jake had some adjusting to do himself.

"Jake, what are we going to do now? How are we going to make this work?" Amanda couldn't help but ask now that they weren't caught up in the heat of passion. Amanda's heart had spoken, but now her mind was buzzing with a million questions.

"I've got most of it figured out, I think," Jake said reassuringly.

"Tell me," Amanda demanded.

"You're looking at the new firearms and defensive tactics instructor for the Los Angeles Field Office," Jake announced.

"You're kidding! I didn't even know we had an opening?" Amanda said in amazement.

"Mark has been trying to get some help out here for quite a while and he mentioned the opportunity to me months ago. Once I said I was interested, the wheels went into motion," Jake explained.

"Why didn't you ever say anything?" Amanda asked, taken aback.

"I didn't want to say anything until I knew for sure the transfer would happen. I was hoping to be able to tell you the day you graduated, but I still hadn't gotten the official offer. Without it, I was afraid it would sound too much like a line that you'd already heard in the past," Jake said, hoping for her understanding.

"Oh Jake. We were way past that already. I wish I had known you felt that strongly."

"Well, if you'd taken any of my phone calls or answered any of my e-mails, I might have told you," Jake said, reprimanding her slightly.

Amanda hung her head, knowing he was right. She had made things difficult.

"You knew I loved you," Jake said softly.

"And I loved you. I just didn't think love was going to be enough. There were too many obstacles that I couldn't see our way around. I was devastated when I got home. I thought it would just be easier to make a clean break," Amanda said, pleading for understanding.

"Did it make it easier?" Jake asked, knowing the answer but wanting to hear it from her anyway.

"You know it didn't," Amanda admitted.

"Is it bad if I say I'm glad?" Jake said with a smile, so happy to see his ring on her finger.

"Yes. It is bad. You must have been planning all this for a while and you didn't say a word," Amanda said in frustration, thinking about how difficult the past six weeks had been.

"How could I? You didn't even want to talk to me. That really hurt," Jake said, thinking back to his own heartache over the situation.

"I'm sorry," Amanda said, feeling genuinely sorry at the extra heartache she'd put them both through.

"What made you still go ahead with all this? You couldn't have known for sure how I still felt," Amanda asked now in wonder, thinking about what it must have been like for him to take this leap of faith.

"Oh, I did," Jake said smugly. "I had a spy who was filling me in on everything."

Amanda thought for a moment and then said, "Mark? That sneak. What was he telling you?"

"All he had to tell me about was Mr. Hippo. Once he mentioned the strange little hippo you had sitting on your desk that you stared at often when you thought no one was watching, I knew you still cared and hadn't just let it all go. Plus, he mentioned you'd been pretty depressed since you'd gotten back from the academy."

"Depressed? I definitely need to have a word with him, don't I? Pretending to be my friend and the whole time he's spying on me for you," Amanda said in mock outrage.

"He is your friend. Never doubt it. He made sure I had only the best of intentions in mind before he agreed to report back to me," Jake said seriously.

"Oh really," Amanda said, thinking back to some of the things she'd shared with Mark recently.

"Yes. He genuinely likes you, you know. I wonder if he wouldn't have eventually made a play for you himself?" Jake teased.

"Ha! I'm not his type," Amanda joked back.

"What? Since when isn't a beautiful woman his type?" Jake said, knowing his friend well.

"Well, actually, he kind of made a play before I even went to the academy," Amanda said laughing.

"What?" Jake asked, momentarily stunned by that statement. He was sure he'd asked them both that very question before and he'd never gotten this answer!

"Yeah. I turned him down though. HE wasn't MY type!" Amanda said, trying to keep a straight face.

"Apparently we both need to have a word with him, don't we?" Jake said, grinning good-naturedly. "I guess I can't really blame the guy though, can I."

"He did try and get me to go on a blind date once, a few weeks after I got back from the academy. It was a set up, wasn't it?" Amanda asked, already guessing the answer.

"Yes. It was all bogus, but I wanted to know what your reaction would be. I'd given the academy a months notice so they could fill my position before I left and I was feeling a little unsure at the monumental risk I was taking," Jake admitted.

"So, my reaction made you feel secure?" Amanda questioned.

"Sure did," Jake answered with a grin. "If I remember correctly, you told Mark not only that you weren't interested, but also that you were swearing off guys for a while. That combined with the fact that Mark said you described the hippo as something special that you'd brought back from the academy. He also said you almost punched him when he dared to toss the hippo up in the air, while he was making fun of the fact that you had a stuffed animal at work," Jake said happily.

"Are you saying Mr. Hippo sealed the deal?" Amanda asked with a laugh.

"Yes I am. He was the best impulse purchase ever!"

"By the way, why did you bring Mr. Hippo into work and not leave him at home? Not that I'm complaining since Mark never would have known about him otherwise," Jake asked curiously.

Amanda turned a little red in embarrassment before answering, "After the first couple days at home when I was hugging him every night and thinking about you instead of sleeping I decided to wean myself slowly. Bringing him to work seemed like a good compromise. I just couldn't bring myself to part with him completely," Amanda admitted, somewhat shyly.

Jake loved that she was being completely honest about it. "Well, I guess we'll have to give that hippo an honored spot in our house forever now, won't we?" Jake said with a groan.

"Yes, we will!" Amanda said laughing.

"Speaking of a house, where are you staying and what's your plan for that?" Amanda asked.

"I just got in last night after driving cross country and I crashed at Mark's place. I was obviously hoping things would go well today and you'd let me move into your place with you," Jake said with a grin.

"Sight unseen?" Amanda asked, thinking of her small apartment fitting the two of them.

"I've got you, don't I? What more do I need? Besides, we can start looking for a house to buy together after we're married," Jake said, not one to sweat the small stuff.

"Back up a step. No way is my mom going to let you move in with me before we're married," Amanda said, that reality just dawning on her.

"OK...we better get married quick then and I'll beg Mark to let me crash at his place a while longer," Jake said with a shrug.

"Are the answers really all that simple?" Amanda asked in amazement, thinking how he'd had an answer for everything so far.

"They can be," Jake said easily and started filling her in on the rest.

"I'm going to be working out of the satellite office in Los Angeles and we'll both be reporting to the same boss. The fact that we won't be working out of the same office will hopefully make our engagement easy to swallow for management. Mark and I are going to head up the new firearms and defensive tactics program together. He's going to start working out of the new satellite office too, starting next week," Jake explained, going over everything he and Mark had been working on the last few weeks.

"Wow. You really do have everything worked out," Amanda said in admiration.

"There are a few things still left--like meeting the parents and planning a wedding," Jake said, making it all sound like no big deal. Amanda marveled at how it all just seemed so easy all of a sudden. What she'd figured was insurmountable, namely their jobs being in different states, was already no longer an issue and everything else seemed simple in comparison.

Jake took Amanda in his arms and kissed her. "How about taking the rest of the week off? I don't have to report in officially until Monday," Jake murmured while nibbling her neck.

"I think that can be arranged," Amanda said, getting goose bumps.

"Grab your stuff and let's go!" Jake said, stopping himself before things could heat up too much more. He couldn't wait to finally be alone with her!

"Let's stop by Mark's office so I can give him a piece of my mind," Amanda said as she was gathering up her things, Mr. Hippo included!

"Definitely. I have a few things to mention to him myself!" Jake said in agreement, knowing that they both just wanted to share the good news with him. "Let's make it quick though," Jake said, eager to get some time alone together.

"Absolutely," Amanda said with that sexy little smile of hers, on the same page as him. She suddenly started feeling all jittery as they were just about to head out the door. "We're really going to do this?" Amanda said, looking down at her engagement ring, still hardly believing all that had transpired.

"Are you ready to become Mrs. Mandy Marshall?"

"I am. Wow. I love the way that sounds!"

Jake grabbed her hand and Amanda pulled open her office door, ready to announce the amazing turn of events to the world.

Stay tuned for Mark Mitchell's story, coming soon in **"NO LIMITATIONS"**

Followed by Tyler "Worthless" Worthington III in **"WITHOUT LIMITS"**

Please join me on Facebook or sign up for my mailing list at SabrinaDevlin.com to be the first to hear about upcoming book releases!